THE FOUR-POOLS MYSTERY

By

JEAN WEBSTER

First published in 1908

This edition published by Read Books Ltd.

British Library Cataloguing-in-Publication Data
A catalogue record for this book is available
from the British Library

CONTENTS

Jean Webster

Alice Jane Chandler Webster, perhaps better known under her pseudonym Jean Webster, was born on 24 July 1876, at Fredonia, New York, USA. She was the eldest child of Annie Moffet Webster and Charles Luther Webster, and spent her early childhood in a strongly matriarchal and activist setting. Her great-grandmother, grandmother and mother all lived under the same roof; her great-grandmother working on temperance issues, and her grandmother on racial equality and women's suffrage. Webster herself remained a lifelong supporter of women's suffrage and children's institutional reform. Alice's mother was niece to Mark Twain, and her father was Twain's business manager and subsequently publisher of many of his books. Unfortunately, the company ran into difficulties, after which her father had a nervous breakdown and leave of absence. He subsequently committed suicide in 1891 from a drug overdose.

Alice attended the Fredonia Normal School and graduated in 1894 in china painting, thereafter attending the Lady Jane Grey School in Binghamton from 1894-96. It was this latter establishment which provided the inspiration for Webster's later novel, *Just Patty* (published 1911). In 1897, Webster entered Vassar College. Majoring in English and economics, she also took courses in welfare and penal reform, and from this point on became heavily involved in improving the living conditions in institutions for delinquent and destitute children. After her graduation in 1901, Webster began writing *When Patty Went to College,* in which she described contemporary women's college life. It was published in 1903, to good reviews, which spurred her on to copmplete her second novel *The Wheat Princess*, published in 1905. In the following years, Webster embarked on an eight month world tour to Burma, China, Egypt, Hong Kong,

India, Indonesia, Japan and Sri Lanka with her friends Ethelyn McKinney, Lena Weinstein and two others, as well as writing *Jerry Junior* in 1907 and *The Four Pools Mystery* in 1908.

Webster's most famous novel, *Daddy-Long-Legs*, was written in less exotic settings however; whilst the author was staying at an old farmhouse in Tyringham, Massachusetts. It tells the story of an orphaned girl, 'Judy' whose attendance at a women's college is sponsored by an anonymous benefactor. The novel takes the form of letters written by the young lady to her sponsor, and met popular and critical acclaim on its release in 1912. Webster later dramatized the work, and spent a substantial amount of time on tour with the play, which starred a young Ruth Chatterton as 'Judy'. In her personal life, Webster was greatly delighted, when, at the age of thirty nine, she was able to marry her long-held love, Glenn Ford McKinney. The marriage had hitherto been prevented due to the expectations of the groom's wealthy and successful father – who had forced the young man into an unhappy marriage with Annette Reynaud. Reynaud and McKinney were granted their divorce in 1915, which meant that he and Webster were able to marry in a quiet ceremony in Washington, Connecticut. They honeymooned in Canada, where they were visited by former president Theodore Roosevelt, who invited himself saying, 'I've always wanted to meet Jean Webster. We can put up a partition in the cabin!' On their return to New York, Webster published *Dear Enemy* (1915), a sequel to *Daddy-Long-Legs*, which also proved to be a bestseller. Later that year, Webster was elated to discover she was pregnant, but was warned the pregnancy might be dangerous due to a history of difficult births in the family. Her friends reported that they had never seen her happier; she suffered severely from morning sickness, but was better by February 1916. She entered the Sloan Hospital for Women, New York on 10 June 1916, and gave birth to a healthy daughter. Unfortunately, despite a positive outlook at first, Webster became ill and died of childbirth fever the following day. Her daughter was named Jean in her honour.

In the Cave

CHAPTER I

INTRODUCING TERRY PATTEN

It was through the Patterson-Pratt forgery case that I first made the acquaintance of Terry Patten, and at the time I should have been more than willing to forego the pleasure.

Our firm rarely dealt with criminal cases, but the Patterson family were long standing clients, and they naturally turned to us when the trouble came. Ordinarily, so important a matter would have been put in the hands of one of the older men, but it happened that I was the one who had drawn up the will for Patterson Senior the night before his suicide, therefore the brunt of the work devolved upon me. The most unpleasant part of the whole affair was the notoriety. Could we have kept it from the papers, it would not have been so bad, but that was a physical impossibility; Terry Patten was on our track, and within a week he had brought down upon us every newspaper in New York.

The first I ever heard of Terry, a card was sent in bearing the inscription, "Mr. Terence K. Patten," and in the lower left-hand corner, "of the Post-Dispatch." I shuddered as I read it. The Post-Dispatch was at that time the yellowest of the yellow journals. While I was still shuddering, Terry walked in through the door the office boy had inadvertently left open.

He nodded a friendly good morning, helped himself to a chair, tossed his hat and gloves upon the table, crossed his legs comfortably, and looked me over. I returned the scrutiny with interest while I was mentally framing a polite formula for getting rid of him without giving rise to any ill feeling. I had no desire to annoy unnecessarily any of the Post-Dispatch's young men.

At first sight my caller did not strike me as unlike a dozen other reporters. His face was the face one feels he has a right to expect of a newspaper man—keen, alert, humorous; on the look-out for opportunities. But with a second glance I commenced to feel interested. I wondered where he had come from and what he had done in the past. His features were undeniably Irish; but that which chiefly awakened my curiosity, was his expression. It was not only wide-awake and intelligent; it was something more. "Knowing" one would say. It carried with it the mark of experience, the indelible stamp of the street. He was a man who has had no childhood, whose education commenced from the cradle.

I did not arrive at all of these conclusions at once, however, for he had finished his inspection before I had fairly started mine. Apparently he found me satisfactory. The smile which had been lurking about the corners of his mouth broadened to a grin, and I commenced wondering uncomfortably what there was funny about my appearance. Then suddenly he leaned forward and began talking in a quick, eager way, that required all my attention to keep abreast of him. After a short preamble in which he set forth his view of the Patterson-Pratt case—and a clearsighted view it was—he commenced asking questions. They were such amazingly impudent questions that they nearly took my breath away. But he asked them in a manner so engagingly innocent that I found myself answering them before I was aware of it. There was a confiding air of *bonne camaraderie* about the fellow which completely put one off one's guard.

At the end of fifteen minutes he was on the inside track of most of my affairs, and was giving me advice through a kindly desire to keep me from getting things in a mess. The situation would have struck me as ludicrous had I stopped to think of it; but it is a fact I have noted since, that, with Terry, one does not appreciate situations until it is too late.

When he had got from me as much information as I possessed, he shook hands cordially, said he was happy to have made my acquaintance, and would try to drop in again some day. After he had gone, and I had had time to review our conversation, I began to grow hot over the matter. I grew hotter still when I read his report in the paper the next morning. I could not understand why I had not kicked him out at first sight, and I sincerely hoped that he would drop in again, that I might avail myself of the opportunity.

He did drop in, and I received him with the utmost cordiality. There was something entirely disarming about Terry's impudence. And so it went. He continued to comment upon the case in the most sensational manner possible, and I railed against him and forgave him with unvarying regularity. In the end we came to be quite friendly over the affair. I found him diverting at a time when I was in need of diversion, though just what attraction he found in me, I have never been able to fathom. It was certainly not that he saw a future source of "stories," for he frankly regarded corporation law as a pursuit devoid of interest. Criminal law was the one branch of the profession for which he felt any respect.

We frequently had lunch together; or breakfast, in his case. His day commenced about noon and lasted till three in the morning. "Well, Terry, what's the news at the morgue today?" I would inquire as we settled ourselves at the table. And Terry would rattle off the details of the latest murder mystery with a cheerfully matter-of-fact air that would have been disgusting had it not been so funny.

It was at this time that I learned his history prior to the days of the Post-Dispatch. He was entirely frank about himself, and if one half of his stories were true, he has achieved some amazing adventures. I strongly suspected at times that the reporting instinct got ahead of the facts, and that he embroidered incidents as he went along.

His father, Terry Senior, had been an Irish politician of considerable ability and some prominence on the East River side of the city. The boy's early education had been picked up in the streets (his father had got the truant officer his position) and it was thorough. Later he had received a more theoretical training in the University of New York, but I think it was his early education which stuck by him longest, and which, in the end, was probably the more useful of the two. Armed with this equipment, it was inevitable that he should develop into a star reporter. Not only did he write his news in an entertaining form, but he first made the news he wrote about. When any sensational crime had been committed which puzzled the police, Terry had an annoying way of solving the mystery himself, and publishing the full particulars in the Post-Dispatch with the glory blatantly attributed to "our reporter." The paper was fully aware that Terence K. Patten was an acquisition to its staff. It had sent him on various commissions to various entertaining quarters of the globe, and in the course of his duty he had encountered experiences. One is forced to admit that he was not always fastidious as to the rôle he played. He had cruised about the Mediterranean as assistant cook on a millionaire's yacht, and had listened to secrets between meals. He had wandered about the country with a monkey and a hand-organ in search of a peddler he suspected of a crime. He had helped along a revolution in South America, and had gone up in a captive war balloon which had broken loose and floated off.

But all this is of no concern at present. I am merely going to chronicle his achievement in one instance—in what he himself has always referred to as the "Four-Pools Mystery." It has already been written up in reporter style as the details came to light from day to day. But a ten-year-old newspaper story is as dead as if it were written on parchment, and since the part Terry played was rather remarkable, and many of the details were at the time suppressed, I think it deserves a more permanent form.

It was through the Patterson-Pratt business by a roundabout way that I got mixed up in the Four-Pools affair. I had been working very hard over the forgery case; I spent every day on it for nine weeks—and nearly every night. I got into the way of lying awake, puzzling over the details, when I should have been sleeping, and that is the sort of work which finishes a man. By the middle of April, when the strain was over, I was as near being a nervous wreck as an ordinarily healthy chap can get.

At this stage my doctor stepped in and ordered a rest in some quiet place out of reach of the New York papers; he suggested a fishing expedition to Cape Cod. I apathetically fell in with the idea, and invited Terry to join me. But he jeered at the notion of finding either pleasure or profit in any such trip. It was too far from the center of crime to contain any interest for Terry.

"Heavens, man! I'd as lief spend a vacation in the middle of the Sahara Desert."

"Oh, the fishing would keep things going," I said.

"Fishing! We'd die of ennui before we had a bite. I'd be murdering you at the end of the first week just for some excitement. If you need a rest—and you are rather seedy—forget all about this Patterson business and plunge into something new. The best rest in the world is a counter-irritant."

This was Terry all over; he himself was utterly devoid of nerves, and he could not appreciate the part they played in a man of normal make-up. My being threatened with nervous prostration he regarded as a joke. His pleasantries rather damped my interest in deep-sea fishing, however, and I cast about for something else. It was at this juncture that I thought of Four-Pools Plantation. "Four-Pools" was the somewhat fantastic name of a stock farm in the Shenandoah Valley, belonging to a great-uncle whom I had not seen since I was a boy.

A few months before, I had had occasion to settle a little legal matter for Colonel Gaylord (he was a colonel by courtesy; so far as I could discover he had never had his hands on a gun except for rabbit shooting) and in the exchange of amenities which followed, he had given me a standing invitation to make the plantation my home whenever I should have occasion to come South. As I had no prospect of leaving New York, I thought nothing of it at the time; but now I determined to take the old gentleman at his word, and spend my enforced vacation in getting acquainted with my Virginia relatives.

This plan struck Terry as just one degree funnier than the fishing expedition. The doctor, however, received the idea with enthusiasm. A farm, he said, with plenty of outdoor life and no excitement, was just the thing I needed. But could he have foreseen the events which were to happen there, I doubt if he would have recommended the place for a nervous man.

CHAPTER II

I ARRIVE AT FOUR-POOLS PLANTATION

As I rolled southward in the train—"jerked" would be a fitter word; the roadbeds of western Virginia are anything but level—I strove to recall my old time impressions of Four-Pools Plantation. It was one of the big plantations in that part of the state, and had always been noted for its hospitality. My vague recollection of the place was a kaleidoscopic vision of music and dancing and laughter, set in the moonlit background of the Shenandoah Valley. I knew, however, that in the eighteen years since my boyhood visit everything had changed.

News had come of my aunt's death, and of Nan's runaway marriage against her father's wishes, and of how she too had died without ever returning home. Poor unhappy Nannie! I was but a boy of twelve when I had seen her last, but she had impressed even my unimpressionable age with a sense of her charm. I had heard that Jeff, the elder of the two boys, had gone completely to the bad, and having broken with his father, had drifted off to no one knew where. This to me was the saddest news of all; Jeff had been the object of my first case of hero worship.

I knew that Colonel Gaylord, now an old man, was living alone with Radnor, who I understood had grown into a fine young fellow, all that his brother had promised. My only remembrance of the Colonel was of a tall dark man who wore riding boots and carried a heavy trainer's whip, and of whom I was very much afraid. My only remembrance of Rad was of a pretty little chap of four, eternally in mischief. It was with a mingled feeling of eagerness and regret that I looked forward to the visit—eagerness to see again the scenes which were so pleasantly associated with my boyhood, and regret that I must renew my memories under such sadly changed conditions.

As I stepped from the train, a tall broad-shouldered young man of twenty-three or thereabouts, came forward to meet me. I should have recognized him for Radnor anywhere, so striking was his resemblance to the brother I had known. He wore a loose flannel shirt and a broad-brimmed felt hat cocked on one side, and he looked so exactly the typical Southern man of the stage that I almost laughed as I greeted him. His welcome was frank and cordial and I liked him from the first. He asked after my health with an amused twinkle in his eyes. Nervous prostration evidently struck him as humorously as it did Terry. Lest I resent his apparent lack of sympathy however, he added, with a hearty whack on my shoulder, that I had come to the right place to get cured.

A drive over sweet smelling country roads behind blooded horses was a new experience to me, fresh from city streets and the rumble of elevated trains. I leaned back with a sigh of content, feeling already as if I had got my boyhood back again.

Radnor enlivened the three miles with stories of the houses we passed and the people who lived in them, and to my law-abiding Northern ears, the recital indubitably smacked of the South. This old gentleman—so Rad called him—had kept an illicit still in his cellar for fifteen years, and it had not been discovered until after his death (of delirium tremens). The young lady who lived in that house—one of the belles of the county—had eloped with the best man on the night before the wedding and the rightful groom had shot himself. The one who lived here had eloped with her father's overseer, and had rowed across the river in the only available boat, leaving her outraged parent on the opposite bank.

I finally burst out laughing.

"Does everyone in the South run away to get married? Don't you ever have any legitimate weddings with cake and rice and old shoes?" As I spoke I remembered Nannie and wondered if I had touched on a delicate subject.

But Radnor returned my laugh.

"We do have a good many elopements," he acknowledged. "Maybe there are more cruel parents in the South." Then he suddenly sobered. "I suppose you remember Nan?" he inquired with an air of hesitation.

"A little," I assented.

"Poor girl!" he said. "I'm afraid she had a pretty tough time. You'd best not mention her to the old gentleman—or Jeff either."

"Does the Colonel still feel hard toward them?"

Radnor frowned slightly.

"He doesn't forgive," he returned.

"What was the trouble with Jeff?" I ventured. "I have never heard any particulars."

"He and my father didn't agree. I don't remember very much about it myself; I was only thirteen when it happened. But I know there was the devil of a row."

"Do you know where he is?" I asked.

Radnor shook his head.

"I sent him some money once or twice, but my father found it out and shut down on my bank account. I've lost track of him lately—he isn't in need of money though. The last I heard he was running a gambling place in Seattle."

"It's a great pity!" I sighed. "He was a fine chap when I knew him."

Radnor echoed my sigh but he did not choose to follow up the subject, and we passed the rest of the way in silence until we turned into the lane that led to Four-Pools. After the manner of many Southern places the house was situated well toward the middle of the large plantation, and entirely out of sight from the road. The private lane which led to it was bordered by a hawthorn hedge, and wound for half a mile or so between pastures and flowering peach orchards. I delightedly breathed in the fresh spring odors, wondering meanwhile how it was that I had let that happy Virginia summer of my boyhood slip so entirely from my mind.

As we rounded a clump of willow trees we came in sight of the house, set on a little rise of ground and approached by a rolling sweep of lawn. It was a good example of colonial—white with green blinds, the broad brick floored veranda, which extended the length of the front, supported by lofty Doric columns. On the south side a huge curved portico bulged out to meet the driveway. Stretching away behind the house was a sleepy box-bordered garden, and behind this, screened by a row of evergreens, were clustered the barns and out-buildings. Some little distance to the left, in a slight hollow and half hidden by an overgrowth of laurels, stood a row of one-story weather-beaten buildings—the old negro cabins, left over from the slave days.

"It's just as I remember it!" I exclaimed delightedly as I noted one familiar object after another. "Nothing has changed."

"Nothing does change in the South," said Radnor, "except the people, and I suppose they change everywhere."

"And those are the deserted negro cabins?" I added, my eye resting on the cluster of gray roofs showing above the shrubbery.

"Just at present they are not so deserted as we should like," he returned with a suggestive undertone in his voice. "You visit the plantation at an interesting time. The Gaylord ha'nt has reappeared."

"The Gaylord ha'nt!" I exclaimed in astonishment. "What on earth is that?"

Radnor laughed.

"One of our godless ancestors once beat a slave to death and his ghost comes back, off and on, to haunt the negro cabins. We hadn't heard anything of him for a good many years and had almost forgotten the story, when last week he reappeared. Devil fires have been seen dancing in the laurels at night, and mysterious moanings have been heard around the cabins. If you have ever had anything to do with negroes, you can know the state our servants are in."

"Well!" said I, "that promises entertainment. I shall look

forward to meeting the ha'nt."

We had reached the house by this time, and as we drew up before the portico the Colonel stood on the top step waiting to welcome me. He was looking much as I remembered him except that his hair had turned from black to white, and his former imperious bearing had become a trifle querulous. I jumped out and grasped his outstretched hand.

"I'm glad to see you, my boy! I'm glad to see you," he said cordially.

My heart warmed toward the old man's "my boy." It had been a good many years since anyone had called me that.

"You've grown since I saw you last," he chuckled, as he led the way into the house through the group of negro servants who had gathered to see me arrive.

My first fleeting glimpse through the open doors told me that it was indeed true, as Radnor had said, nothing had changed. The furniture was the same old-fashioned, solidly simple furniture that the house had contained since it was built. I was amused to see the Colonel's gloves and whip thrown carelessly on a chair in the hall. The whip was the one token by which I remembered him.

"So you've been working too hard, have you, Arnold?" the old man inquired, looking me over with twinkling eyes. "We'll give you something to do that will make you forget you've ever seen work before! There are half a dozen colts in the pasture just spoiling to be broken in; you may try your hand at that, sir. And now I reckon supper's about ready," he added. "Nancy doesn't allow any loitering when it's a question of beat biscuits. Take him up to his room, Rad—and you Mose," he called to one of the negroes hanging about the portico, "come and carry up Marse Arnold's things."

At this one of them shambled forward and began picking up my traps which had been dumped in a pile on the steps. His appearance struck me with such an instant feeling of repugnance, that even after I was used to the fellow, I never quite overcame that first involuntary shudder. He was not a full-blooded negro but an octoroon. His color was a muddy yellow, his features were sharp instead of flat, and his hair hung across his forehead almost straight. But these facts alone did not account for his queerness; the most uncanny thing about him was the color of his eyes. They had a yellow glint and narrowed in the light. The creature was bare-footed and wore a faded suit of linsey-woolsey; I wondered at that, for the other servants who had crowded out to see me, were dressed in very decent livery.

Radnor noticed my surprise, and remarked as he led the way up the winding staircase, "Mose isn't much of a beauty, for a fact."

I made no reply as the man was close behind, and the feeling that his eyes were boring into the middle of my back was far from pleasant. But after he had deposited his load on the floor of my room, and, with a sidewise glance which seemed to take in everything without looking directly at anything, had shambled off again, I turned to Rad.

"What's the matter with him?" I demanded.

Radnor threw back his head and laughed.

"You look as if you'd seen the ha'nt! There's nothing to be afraid of. He doesn't bite. The poor fellow's half witted—at least in some respects; in others he's doubly witted."

"Who is he?" I persisted. "Where did he come from?"

"Oh, he's lived here all his life—raised on the place. We're as fond of Mose as if he were a member of the family. He's my father's body servant and he follows him around like a dog. We don't keep him dressed for the part because shoes and stockings make him unhappy."

"But his eyes," I said. "What the deuce is the matter with his eyes?"

Radnor shrugged his shoulders.

"Born that way. His eyes *are* a little queer, but if you've ever noticed it, niggers' eyes are often yellow. The people on the place call him 'Cat-Eye Mose.' You needn't be afraid of him," he added with another laugh, "he's harmless."

CHAPTER III

I MAKE THE ACQUAINTANCE OF THE HA'NT

We had a sensation at supper that night, and I commenced to realize that I was a good many miles from New York. In response to the invitation of Solomon, the old negro butler, we seated ourselves at the table and commenced on the cold dishes before us, while he withdrew to bring in the hot things from the kitchen. As is often the case in Southern plantation houses the kitchen was under a separate roof from the main house, and connected with it by a long open gallery. We waited some time but no supper arrived. The Colonel, becoming impatient, was on the point of going to look for it, when the door burst open and Solomon appeared empty-handed, every hair on his woolly head pointing a different direction.

"De ha'nt, Marse Cunnel, de ha'nt! He's sperrited off de chicken. Right outen de oven from under Nancy's eyes."

"Solomon," said the Colonel severely, "what are you trying to say? Talk sense."

"Sho's yuh bohn, Marse Cunnel; it's de libbin' truf I's tellin' yuh. Dat ha'nt has fotched dat chicken right outen de oven, an' it's vanished in de air."

"You go out and bring that chicken in and don't let me hear another word."

"I cayn't, Marse Cunnel, 'deed I cayn't. Dere ain't no chicken dere."

"Very well, then! Go and get us some ham and eggs and stop this fuss."

Solomon withdrew and we three looked at each other.

"Rad, what's the meaning of this?" the Colonel demanded querulously.

"Some foolishness on the part of the niggers. I'll look into it after supper. When the ha'nt begins abstracting chickens from the oven I think it's time to investigate."

Being naturally curious over the matter, I commenced asking questions about the history and prior appearances of the ha'nt. Radnor answered readily enough, but I noticed that the Colonel appeared restless under the inquiry, and the amused suspicion crossed my mind that he did not entirely discredit the story. When a man has been born and brought up among negroes he comes, in spite of himself, to be tinged with their ideas.

Supper finished, the three of us turned down the gallery toward the kitchen. As we approached the door we heard a murmur of voices, one rising every now and then in a shrill wail which furnished a sort of chorus. Radnor whispered in my ear that he reckoned Nancy had "got um" again. Though I did not comprehend at the moment, I subsequently learned that "um" referred to a sort of emotional ecstasy into which Nancy occasionally worked herself, the motive power being indifferently ghosts or religion.

The kitchen was a large square room, with brick floor, rough shack walls and smoky rafters overhead from which pended strings of garlic, red peppers and herbs. The light was supplied ostensibly by two tallow dips, but in reality by the glowing wood embers of the great open stove bricked into one side of the wall.

Five or six excited negroes were grouped in a circle about a woman with a yellow turban on her head, who was rocking back and forth and shouting at intervals:

"Oh-h, dere's sperrits in de air! I can smell um. I can smell um."

"Nancy!" called the Colonel sharply as we stepped into the room.

Nancy paused a moment and turned upon us a pair of frenzied eyes with nothing much but the whites showing.

"Marse Cunnel, dere's sperrits in de air," she cried. "Sabe yuhself while dere's time. We's all a-treadin' de road to destruction."

"You'll be treading the road to destruction in mighty short order if you don't keep still," he returned grimly. "Now stop this foolishness and tell me what's gone with that chicken."

After a great deal of questioning and patching together, we finally got her story, but I cannot say that it threw much light upon the matter. She had put the chicken in the oven, and then she felt powerful queer, as if something were going to happen. Suddenly she felt a cold wind blow through the room, the candles went out, and she could hear the rustle of "ghostly gahments" sweeping past her. The oven door sprang open of its own accord; she looked inside, and "dere wa'n't no chicken dere!"

Repeated questioning only brought out the same statement but with more circumstantial details. The other negroes backed her up, and the story grew rapidly in magnitude and horror. Nancy's seizures, it appeared, were contagious, and the others by this time were almost as excited as she. The only approximately calm one among them was Cat-Eye Mose who sat in the doorway watching the scene with half furtive eyes and something resembling a grin on his face.

The Colonel, observing that it was a good deal of commotion for the sake of one small chicken, disgustedly dropped the inquiry. As we stepped out into the gallery again, I glanced back at the dancing firelight, the weird cross shadows, and the circle of dusky faces, with, I confess, a somewhat creepy feeling. I could see that in such an atmosphere, it would not take long for superstition to lay its hold on a man.

"What's the meaning of it?" I asked as we strolled slowly toward the house.

"The meaning of it," Radnor shrugged, "is that some of them are lying. The ha'nt, I could swear, has a good flesh and blood appetite. Nancy has been frightened and she believes her own story. There's never any use in trying to sift a negro's lies; they have so much imagination that after five minutes they believe themselves."

"I think I could spot the ghost," I returned. "And that's your precious Cat-Eye Mose."

Radnor shook his head.

"Mose doesn't need to steal chickens. He gets all he wants."

"Mose," the Colonel added emphatically, "is the one person on the place who is absolutely to be trusted."

We had almost reached the house, when we were suddenly startled by a series of shrieks and screams coming toward us across the open stretch of lawn that lay between us and the old negro cabins. In another moment an old woman, her face twitching with terror, had thrown herself at our feet in a species of convulsion.

"De ha'nt! De ha'nt! He's a-beckoning," was all we could make out between her moans.

The other negroes came pouring out from the kitchen and gathered in a frenzied circle about the writhing woman. Mose, I noted, was among them; he could at least prove an alibi this time.

"Here Mose, quick! Get us some torches," Radnor called. "We'll fetch that ha'nt up here to answer for himself.—It's old Aunt Sukie," he added to me, nodding toward the woman on the ground whose spasms by this time were growing somewhat quieter. "She lives on the next plantation and was probably taking a cross cut through the laurel path that leads by the cabins. She's almost a hundred and is pretty nearly a witch herself."

Mose shambled up with some torches—pine knots dipped in tar, such as they used for hunting 'possums at night, and he and I and Radnor set out for the cabins. I noticed that none of the other negroes volunteered to assist; I also noticed that Mose went on ahead with a low whining cry which sent chills chasing up and down my back.

"What's the matter with him?" I gasped, more intent on the negro than the ghost we had come to search.

"That's the way he always hunts," Radnor laughed. "There are a good many things about Mose that you will have to get used to."

We searched the whole region of the abandoned quarters

with a considerable degree of thoroughness. Three or four of the larger cabins were used as store houses for fodder; the rest were empty. We poked into all of them, but found nothing more terrifying than a few bats and owls. Though I did not give much consideration to the fact at the time, I later remembered that there was one of the cabins which we didn't explore as thoroughly as the rest. Mose dropped his torch as we entered, and in the confusion of relighting it, the interior was somewhat slighted. In any case we unearthed no ha'nt that night; and we finally gave up the search and turned back to the house.

"I suspect," Radnor laughed, "that if the truth were known, old Aunt Sukie's beckoning ha'nt would turn out to be nothing more alarming than a white cow waving her tail."

"It's rather suggestive coming on top of the chicken episode," I observed.

"Oh, this won't be the end! We'll have ha'nt served for breakfast, dinner and supper during the rest of your stay. When the niggers begin to see things they keep it up."

When I went upstairs that night, Rad followed close on my heels to see that I had everything I needed. The room was a huge four windowed affair, furnished with a canopied bed and a mahogany wardrobe as big as a small house. The nights still being chilly, a roaring wood fire had been built, adding a note of cheerfulness to an otherwise sombre apartment.

"This was Nan's room," he said suddenly.

"Nan's room!" I echoed glancing about the shadowy interior. "Rather heavy for a girl."

"It is a trifle severe," he agreed, "but I dare say it was different when she was here. Her things are all packed away in the attic." He picked up a candle and held it so that it lighted the face of a portrait over the mantle. "That's Nan—painted when she was eighteen."

"Yes," I nodded. "I recognized her the moment I saw it. She was like that when I knew her."

"It used to hang down stairs but after her marriage my father had it brought up here. He kept the door locked until the news came that she was dead, then he turned it into a guest room. He never comes in himself; he won't look at the picture."

Radnor spoke shortly, but with an underlying note of bitterness. I could see that he felt keenly on the subject. After a few desultory words, he somewhat brusquely said good night, and left me to the memories of the place.

Instead of going to bed I set about unpacking. I was tired but wide awake. Aunt Sukie's convulsions and our torch light hunt for ghosts were novel events in my experience, and they acted as anything but a sedative. The unpacking finished, I settled myself in an easy chair before the fire and fell to studying the portrait. It was a huge canvas in the romantic fashion of Romney, with a landscape in the background. The girl was dressed in flowing pink drapery, a garden hat filled with roses swinging from her arm, a Scotch collie with great lustrous eyes pressed against her side. The pose, the attributes, were artificial; but the painter had caught the spirit. Nannie's face looked out of the frame as I remembered it from long ago. Youth and gaiety and goodness trembled on her lips and laughed in her eyes. The picture seemed a prophecy of all the happiness the future was to bring. Nannie at eighteen with life before her!

And three years later she was dying in a dreary little Western town, separated from her girlhood friends, without a word of forgiveness from her father. What had she done to deserve this fate? Merely set up her will against his, and married the man she loved. Her husband was poor, but from all I ever heard, a very decent chap. As I studied the eager smiling face, I felt a hot wave of anger against her father. What a power of vindictiveness the man must have, still to cherish rancour against a daughter fifteen years in her grave! There was something too poignantly sad about the unfulfilled hope of the picture. I blew out the candles to rid my mind of poor little Nannie's smile.

I sat for some time my eyes fixed moodily on the glowing embers, till I was roused by the deep boom of the hall clock as it slowly counted twelve. I rose with a laugh and a yawn. The first of the doctor's orders had been, "Early to bed!" I hastily made ready, but before turning in, paused for a moment by the open window, enticed by the fresh country smells of plowed land and sprouting green things, that blew in on the damp breeze. It was a wild night with a young moon hanging low in the sky. Shadows chased themselves over the lawn and the trees waved and shifted in the wind. It had been a long time since I had looked out on such a scene of peaceful tranquillity as this. New York with the hurry and rush of its streets, with the horrors of Terry's morgue, seemed to lie in another continent.

But suddenly I was recalled to the present by hearing, almost beneath me, the low shuddering squeak of an opening window. I leaned out silently alert, and to my surprise I saw Cat-Eye Mose—though it was pretty dark I could not be mistaken in his long loping run—slink out from the shadow of the house and make across the open space of lawn toward the deserted negro cabins. As he ran he was bent almost double over a large black bundle which he carried in his arms. Though I strained my eyes to follow him I could make out nothing more before he had plunged into the shadow of the laurels.

CHAPTER IV

THE HA'NT GROWS MYSTERIOUS

I waked early and hurried through with my dressing, eager to get down stairs and report my last night's finding in regard to Mose. My first impulse had been to rouse the house, but on soberer second thoughts I had decided to wait till morning. I was glad now that I had; for with the sunlight streaming in through the eastern windows, with the fresh breeze bringing the sound of twittering birds, life seemed a more cheerful affair than it had the night before, and the whole aspect of the ha'nt took on a distinctly humorous tone.

A ghost who wafted roast chickens through the air and out of doors on a breeze of its own constructing, appealed to me as having an original mind. Since my midnight discovery I felt pretty certain that I could identify the ghost; and as I recalled the masterly way in which Mose had led and directed the hunt, I decided that he was cleverer than Rad had given him credit for. I went down stairs with my eyes and ears wide open prepared for further revelations. The problems of my profession had never led me into any consideration of the supernatural, and the rather evanescent business of hunting down a ha'nt came as a welcome contrast to the very material details of my recent forgery case. I had found what Terry would call a counter-irritant.

It was still early, and neither the Colonel nor Radnor had appeared; but Solomon was sweeping off the portico steps and I addressed myself to him. He was rather coy at first about discussing the matter of the ha'nt, as he scented my scepticism, but in the end he volunteered:

"Some says de ha'nt's a woman dat one o' de Gaylords long time ago, should o' married an' didn't, an' dat pined away an' died. An' some says it's a black man one o' dem whupped to deaf."

"Which do you think it is?" I inquired.

"Bress yuh, Marse Arnold, I ain't thinkin' nuffen. Like es not hit's bofe. When one sperrit gits oneasy 'pears like he stir up all de odders. Dey gets so lonely like lyin' all by dereselves in de grave dat dey're 'most crazy for company. An' when dey cayn't get each odder dey'll take humans. De human what's consorted wid a gohs, Marse Arnold, he's nebber hisself no moah. He's sort uh half-minded like Mose."

"Is that what's the matter with Mose?" I pursued tentatively. "Does he consort with ghosts?"

"Mose was bawn dat way, but I reckon maybe dat was what was de matter wid his mudder, an' he cotched it."

"That was rather an unusual thing, last night, wasn't it, for a ha'nt to steal a chicken?"

"'Pears like ha'nts must have dere jokes like odder folkses," was as far as Solomon would go.

At breakfast I repeated what I had seen the night before, and to my indignation both Radnor and my uncle took it calmly.

"Mose is only a poor half witted fellow but he's as honest as the day," the Colonel declared, "and I won't have him turned into a villain for your entertainment."

"He may be honest," I persisted, "but just the same he knows what became of that chicken! And what's more, if you look about the house you'll find there's something else missing."

The Colonel laughed good-naturedly.

"If it raises your suspicions to have Mose prowling around in the night, you'll have to get used to suspicions; for you'll have 'em during the rest of your stay. I've known Mose to stop out in the woods for three nights running—he's as much an animal as he is a man; but he's a tame animal, and you needn't be afraid of him. If you'd followed him and his bundle last night I reckon you'd have made a mighty queer discovery. He has his own little amusements and they aren't exactly ours, but since he doesn't hurt anybody what's the use in bothering? I've known Mose for well on to thirty years, and I've never yet known him to do a meanness to any human being. There aren't many white folks I can say the same of."

I did not pursue the subject with the Colonel, but I later suggested to Rad that we continue our investigation. He echoed his father's laugh. If we set out to investigate all the imaginings that came into the niggers' heads we should have our hands full, was his reply. I dropped the matter for the time being, but I was none the less convinced that Mose and the ghost were near relations; and I determined to keep an eye on him in the future, at least in so far as one could keep an eye on so slippery an individual.

In pursuance of this design, I took the opportunity that first morning, while Rad and his father were engaged with the veterinary surgeon who had come to doctor a sick colt, of strolling in the direction of the deserted cabins.

It was a damp malarious looking spot, though I dare say in the old days when the land was drained, it had been healthy enough. Just below the cabins lay the largest of the four pools which gave the plantation its name. The other three lying in the pastures higher up were used for watering the stock and were kept clean and free from plant growth. But the lower pool, abandoned like the cabins, had been allowed to overflow its banks until it was completely surrounded with rushes and lily pads. A rank growth of willow trees hung over the water and shut out all but the merest glint of sunlight.

Above this pool the cabins stretched in a double row occupying the base of the declivity on which the "big house" stood. There were as many as a dozen, I should think, built of logs and unpainted shack, consisting for the most part of a single large room, though a few had a loft above and a rough lean-to in the rear. A walk bordered by laurels stretched down the center between the two rows, and as the trees had not been clipped for a good many years, the shade was somewhat sombre. Add to this the fact that one or two of the roofs had fallen in, that the hinges were missing from several doors, that there was not a whole pane of glass in all the dozen cabins, and it will readily be seen that the place gave rise to no very cheerful fancies. I wondered that the Colonel did not have the houses pulled down; they were not a souvenir of past times which I myself should have cared to preserve.

The damp earth where the shade was thickest, plainly showed the marks of foot-prints—some made by bare feet, some by shoes—but I could not follow them for more than a yard or so, and I could not be certain they were not our own traces of the night before. I poked into every one of the cabins, but found nothing suspicious about their appearance. I did not, to be sure, ascend to any of the half dozen lofts, as there were no stairs and no suggestion of a ladder anywhere about. The open traps however which led to them were so thickly festooned with spider webs and dirt, that it did not seem possible that anyone had passed through for a dozen years. Finding no sign of habitation, either human or spiritual, I finally turned back to the house with a philosophic shrug and the reflection that Cat-Eye Mose's nocturnal vagaries were no affair of mine.

During the next few days we in the front part of the house heard only faint echoes of the excitement, though I believe that the ha'nt, both past and present, was the chief topic of conversation among the negroes, not only at Four-Pools but among the neighboring plantations as well. I spent my time those first few days in getting acquainted with my new surroundings. The chief business of the farm was horse raising, and the Colonel kept a well stocked stable. A riding horse was put at my disposal, and in company with Radnor I explored the greater part of the valley.

We visited at a number of houses in the neighborhood, but there was one in particular where we stopped most frequently, and it did not take me long to discover the reason. "Mathers Hall", an ivy-covered rambling structure, red brick with white trimmings—in style half colonial, half old English—was situated a mile or so from Four-Pools. The Hall had sheltered three generations of Matherses, and the fourth generation was growing up. There was a huge family, mostly girls, who had married and moved away to Washington or Richmond or Baltimore. They all came back in the summer however bringing their babies with them, and the place was the center of gaiety in the neighborhood. There was just one unmarried daughter left—Polly, nineteen years old, and the most heartlessly charming young person it has ever been my misfortune to meet. As is likely to be the case with the baby of a large family, Polly was thoroughly spoiled, but that fact did not in the least diminish her charm.

Report had it, at the time of my arrival, that after refusing every marriageable man in the county, she was now trying to make up her mind between Jim Mattison and Radnor. Whether or not these statistics were exaggerated, I cannot say, but in any case the many other aspirants for her favor had tacitly dropped out of the running, and the race was clearly between the two.

It seemed to me, had I been Polly, that it would not take me long to decide. Rad was as likable a young fellow as one would ever meet; he came from one of the best families in the county, with the prospect of inheriting at his father's death a very fair sized fortune. It struck me that a girl would have to search a good while before discovering an equally desirable husband. But I was surprised to find that this was not the general opinion in the neighborhood. Radnor's reputation, I learned with something of a shock, was far from what it should have been. I was told with a meaning undertone that he "favored" his brother Jeff. Though many of the stories were doubtless exaggerated, I learned subsequently that there was too much truth in some of them. It was openly said that Polly Mathers would be doing a great deal better if she chose young Mattison, for though he might not have the prospect of as much money as Radnor Gaylord, he was infinitely the steadier of the two. Mattison was a good-looking and rather ill-natured young giant, but it did not strike me at the time, nor later in the light of succeeding events, that he was particularly endowed with brains. By way of occupation, he was described as being in "politics"; at that time he was sheriff of the county, and was fully aware of the importance of the office.

I fear that Polly had a good deal of the coquette in her make-up, and she thoroughly enjoyed the jealousy between the two young men. Whenever Radnor by any chance incurred her displeasure, she retaliated by transferring her smiles to Mattison; and the virtuous young sheriff took good care that if Rad committed any slips, Polly should hear of them. As a result, they succeeded in keeping his temper in a very inflammable state.

I had not been long at Four-Pools before I commenced to see that there was an undercurrent to the life of the household which I had not at first suspected. The Colonel had grown strict as he grew old; his experience with his elder son had made him bitter, and he did not adopt the most diplomatic way of dealing with Radnor. The boy had inherited a good share of his father's stubborn temper and indomitable will; the two, living alone, inevitably clashed. Radnor at times seemed possessed of the very devil of perversity; and if he ever drank or gambled, it was as much to assert his independence as for any other reason. There were days when he and his father were barely on speaking terms.

Life at the plantation, however, was for the most part easy-going and flexible, as is likely to be the case in a bachelor establishment. We dropped cigar ashes anywhere we pleased, cocked our feet on the parlor table if we saw fit, and let the dogs troop all over the place. I spent the greater part of my time on horseback, riding about the country with Radnor on business for the farm. He, I soon discovered, did most of the actual work, though his father was still the nominal head of affairs. The raising of thoroughbreds is no longer the lucrative business that it used to be, and it required a good manager to bring the balance out on the right side of the ledger. Rad was such a spectacular looking young fellow that I was really surprised to find what sound business judgment he possessed. He insisted upon introducing modern methods where his father would have been content to drift along in the casual manner of the old South, and his clear-sightedness more than doubled the income of the place.

In the healthy out-of-door life I soon forgot that nerves existed. The only thing which at all marred the enjoyment of those first few days was the knowledge of occasional clashings between Radnor and his father. I think that they were both rather ashamed of these outbreaks, and I noticed that they tried to conceal the fact from me by an elaborate if somewhat stiff courtesy toward each other.

In order to make clear the puzzling series of events which followed, I must go back to, I believe, the fifth night of my arrival. Radnor was giving a dance at Four-Pools for the purpose, he said, of introducing me into society; though as a matter of fact Polly Mathers was the guest of honor. In any case the party was given, and everyone in the neighborhood (the term "neighborhood" is broad in Virginia; it describes a ten mile radius) both young and old came in carriages or on horseback; the younger ones to dance half the night, the older ones to play cards and look on. I met a great many pretty girls that evening—the South deserves its reputation—but Polly Mathers was by far the prettiest; and the contest for her favors between Radnor and young Mattison was spirited and open. Had Rad consulted his private wishes, the sheriff would not have been among the guests.

It was getting on toward the end of the evening and the musicians, a band of negro fiddlers made up from the different plantations, were resting after a Virginia reel that had been more a romp than a dance, when someone—I think it was Polly herself—suggested that the company adjourn to the laurel walk to see if the ha'nt were visible. The story of old Aunt Sukie's convulsions and of the spirited roast chicken had spread through the countryside, and there had been a good many laughing allusions to it during the evening. Running upstairs in search of a hat I met Rad on the landing, buttoning something white inside his coat, something that to my eyes looked suspiciously like a sheet. He laughed and put his finger on his lips as he went on down to join the others.

It was a bright moonlight night almost as light as day. We moved across the open lawn in a fairly compact body. The girls, though they had been laughing all the evening at the exploits of the ha'nt, showed a cautious tendency to keep on the inside. Rad was in the front ranks leading the hunt, but I noticed as we entered the shrubbery that he disappeared among the shadows, and I for one was fairly certain that our search would be rewarded. We paused in a group at the nearer end of the row of cabins and stood waiting for the ha'nt to show himself. He was obliging. Four or five minutes, and a faint flutter of white appeared in the distance at the farther end of the laurel walk. Then as we stood with expectant eyes fixed on the spot, we saw a tall white figure sway across a patch of moonlight with a beckoning gesture in our direction, while the breeze bore a faintly whispered, "Come! Come!" We were none of us overbold; our faith was not strong enough to run the risk of spoiling the illusion. With shrieks and laughter we turned and made helter-skelter for the house, breaking in among the elder members of the party with the panting announcement, "We've seen the ha'nt!"

Polly loitered on the veranda while supper was being served, waiting, I suspect for Radnor to reappear. I joined her, very willing indeed that the young man should delay. Polly, her white dress gleaming in the moonlight, her eyes filled with laughter, her cheeks glowing with excitement, was the most entrancing little creature I have ever seen. She was so bubbling over with youth and light-heartedness that I felt, in contrast, as if I were already tottering on the brink of the grave. I was just thirty that summer, but if I live to be a hundred I shall never feel so old again.

"Well Solomon," I remarked as I helped myself to some cakes he was passing, "we've been consorting with ghosts tonight."

"I reckon dis yere gohs would answer to de name o' Marse Radnah," said Solomon, with a wise shake of his head. "But just de same it ain't safe to mock at ha'nts. Dey'll get it back at you when you ain't expectin' it!"

After an intermission of half an hour or so the music commenced again, but still no Radnor. Polly cast more than one glance in the direction of the laurels and the sparkle in her eyes grew ominous. Presently young Mattison appeared in the doorway and asked her to come in and dance, but she said that she was tired, and we three stood laughing and chatting for some ten minutes longer, when a step suddenly sounded on the gravel path and Radnor rounded the corner of the house. As the bright moonlight fell on his face, I stared at him in astonishment. He was pale to his very lips and there were strained anxious lines beneath his eyes.

"What's the matter, Radnor?" Polly cried. "You look as if you'd found the ha'nt!"

He made an effort at composure and laughed in return, though to my ears the laugh sounded very hollow.

"I believe this is my dance, isn't it, Polly?" he asked, joining us with rather an over-acted air of carelessness.

"Your dance was over half an hour ago," Polly returned. "This is Mr. Mattison's."

She turned indoors with the young man, and Rad following on their heels, made his way to the punch bowl where I saw him toss off three or four glasses with no visible interval between them. I, decidedly puzzled, watched him for the rest of the evening. He appeared to have some disturbing matter on his mind, and his gaiety was clearly forced.

It was well on toward morning when the party broke up, and after some slight conversation of a desultory sort the Colonel, Rad and I went up to our rooms. Whether it was the excitement of the evening or the coffee I had drunk, in any case I was not sleepy. I turned in, only to lie for an hour or more with my eyes wide open staring at a patch of moonlight on the ceiling. My old trouble of insomnia had overtaken me again. I finally rose and paced the floor in sheer desperation, and then paused to stare out of the window at the peaceful moonlit picture before me.

Suddenly I heard, as on the night of my arrival, the soft creaking of the French window in the library, which opened on to the veranda just below me. Quickly alert, I leaned forward determined to learn if possible the reason for Mose's midnight wanderings. To my astonishment it was Radnor who stepped out from the shadow of the house, carrying a large black bundle in his arms. I clutched the frame of the window and stared after him in dumb amazement, as he crossed the strip of moonlit lawn and plunged into the shadows of the laurel growth.

CHAPTER V

CAT-EYE MOSE CREATES A SENSATION

For the next week or so things went rather strangely on the plantation. I knew very well that there was an undercurrent of which I was supposed to know nothing, and I appeared politely unconscious; but I won't say but that I kept my eyes and ears as wide open as was possible without appearing to spy. The chicken episode and Aunt Sukie's convulsions turned out to be only the beginning of the ha'nt excitement; scarcely a day passed without some fresh supernatural visitation. Radnor pooh-poohed over the matter before the Colonel and me, but with the negroes I know that he encouraged rather than discouraged their fears, until there was not a man on our own or any of the neighboring plantations who would have ventured to step foot within the laurel walk, either at night or in the daytime—at least there was only one. Cat-Eye Mose took the matter of the ha'nt without undue emotion, a point which struck me as suggestive, for I knew that Mose was as superstitious as the rest when the occasion warranted.

Once at least I saw Radnor and Mose in consultation, and though I did not know the subject of the conference my suspicions were very near the surface. I came upon them in the stables talking in low tones, Rad apparently explaining, and Mose listening with the air of strained attention which the slightest mental effort always called to his face. At my appearance Radnor raised his voice and added one or two directions as to how his guns were to be cleaned. It was evident that the subject had been changed.

Everything that was missing about the place—and there seemed to be an abnormal amount—was attributed to the ha'nt. I do not doubt but that the servants made the ha'nt a convenient scapegoat to answer for their own shortcomings, but still there were several suggestive depredations—horse blankets from the stable, clothes from the line and more edibles than roast chicken from Nancy's larder. The climax of absurdity was reached when there disappeared a rather trashy French novel, which I had left in the summer house. I asked Solomon about it, thinking that one of the servants might have brought it in. Solomon rolled his eyes and suggested that the ha'nt had cotched it. I laughingly commented upon the occurrence at the supper table and the next day Rad handed me the book; Mose had found it, he said, and had brought it up to his room.

All of these minor occurrences were stretched over a period of, say ten days after the party, and though it gave me the uncomfortable feeling that there was something in the air which I did not understand, I did not let it worry me unduly. Radnor seemed to be on the inside track of whatever was going on, and he was old enough to take care of his own affairs. I knew that he had more than once visited the laurel walk after the house was supposed to be asleep; but I kept this knowledge to myself, and allowed no hint to reach the Colonel.

I had, during these first few weeks, all the opportunity I wished of studying Mose's character. Radnor was occupied a good deal of the time—spring on a big river plantation is a busy season—and as I had professed myself fond of shooting, the Colonel turned me over to the care of Cat-Eye Mose. Had I myself been choosing, I should have selected another guide. But Mose was the best hunter on the place, and as the Colonel was quite untroubled by his vagaries, it never occurred to him that I might not be equally confident. In time I grew used to the fellow, but I will admit that at first I accepted his services with some honest trepidation. As I watched him going ahead of me, crouching behind bushes, springing from hummock to hummock, silent and alert, quivering like an animal in search of prey, my attention was centered on him rather than on any possible quarry.

I shall never forget running across him in the woods one afternoon when I had gone out snipe shooting alone. Whether he had followed me or whether we had chosen the same vicinity by chance, I do not know; but at any rate as I came out from the underbrush on the edge of a low, swampy place, I almost stepped on the man. He was stretched face downward on the black, oozy soil with his arm buried in a hole at the foot of a tree.

"Why Mose!" I cried in amazement, "what on earth are you doing here?"

He responded without raising his head.

"I's aftah a snake, sah. I see a big fat gahtah snake a-lopin' into dis yere hole, an' he's skulkin' dar now thinkin' like he gwine to fool me. But he cayn't do dat, sah. I's got 'im by de tail, an' I'll fotch 'im out."

He drew forth as he spoke a huge black and yellow snake, writhing and hissing, and proceeded to smash its head with a stone. I shut my eyes during the operation and when I opened them again I saw to my horror that he was stuffing the carcass in the front of his shirt.

"Good heavens, Mose!" I cried, aghast. "What are you going to do with that?"

"Boil it into oil, sah, to scar de witches off."

Inquiry at the house that night brought out the fact that this was one of Mose's regular occupations. Snake's oil was in general favor among the negroes as a specific against witches, and Mose was the chief purveyor of the lotion. Taken all in all he was about as queer a human being as I have ever come across, and I fancy, had I been a psychologist instead of a lawyer, I might have found him an entertaining study.

I heard about this time some fresh rumors in regard to Radnor; one—and it came pretty straight—that he'd just lost a hundred dollars at poker. A hundred dollars may not sound like a very big loss in these days of bridge, but it was large for that place, and it represented to Radnor exactly two months' pay. As overseer of the plantation, the Colonel paid him six hundred dollars a year, a little enough sum considering the work he did. Rad had nothing in his own right; aside from his salary he was entirely dependent on his father, and it struck me as more than foolish for a young man who was contemplating marriage to throw away two months' earnings in a single game of poker. The conviction crossed my mind that perhaps after all Polly was wise to delay.

I heard another rumor however which was graver than the poker affair; it was only a rumor, and when traced to its source turned out to be nothing more tangible than somebody's hazarded guess, but without the slightest cause the same suspicion had already presented itself to me. And that was, that the ha'nt was a very flesh and blood woman. Radnor was clearly in some sort of trouble; he was moody and irritable, so sharp with the farm hands that several of them left, and unusually taciturn with the Colonel and me. To make matters worse Polly Mathers was treating him with marked indifference, and openly bestowing her smiles upon Mattison; what the trouble was I could only conjecture, but I feared that she too had been hearing rumors.

The ha'nt stories had been repeated and exaggerated until they contained no semblance of truth. By this time, not only the laurel walk was haunted, but the spring-hole as well; and it soon became a region of even greater fear than the deserted cabins. The "spring-hole" was a natural cavity in the side of a hill a half mile or so back from the house. It was out of this cavity that the underground stream flowed which fed the pools, and furnished such valuable irrigation to the place. All that part of Virginia is undermined with limestone caverns, and my uncle's was by no means the only plantation that could boast the distinction of a private cave. The entrance was half hidden among rugged piled-up boulders dripping with moisture; and was not inviting. I remembered chasing a rabbit into this cavern when I was a boy, and though it would have been an easy matter to follow him,

I preferred to stay outside in the sunshine. The spring-hole, then, was haunted. This did not strike me as strange. I rather wondered that it had not been from the first; it was a likely place for ghosts. But the thing which did surprise me, was the fact that it was Mose who brought the news.

We were sitting on the portico after supper one night—it was almost dark and the glow from our cigars was the one visible point in the scenery—when Mose came bounding across the lawn with his peculiar loping run and fairly groveled at Radnor's feet, his teeth chattering with fear.

"I's seen de ha'nt, Marse Rad; de sho nuff ha'nt all dressed in black an' risin' outen de spring-hole."

"You fool!" Radnor cried. "Get on your feet and behave yourself."

"It was de debbil," Mose chattered. "His face was black an' his eyes was fire."

"You've been drinking, Mose," Radnor said sharply. "Get off to the quarters where you belong, and don't let me see you again until you are sober," and he shunted the fellow out of the way before he had time to say any more.

I myself was tolerably certain that Mose had not been drinking; that, at least, was not in the list of his peculiar vices. He appeared to be thoroughly frightened—if not, he was a most consummate actor. In the light of what I already knew, I was considerably puzzled by this fresh manifestation. The Colonel fretted and fumed up and down the veranda, muttering something about these fool niggers all being alike. He had bragged considerably about Mose's immunity in respect to ha'nts, and I think he was rather dashed at his favorite's falling-off. I held my peace, and Radnor returned in a few minutes.

"Rad," said the Colonel, "this thing's going too far. The whole place is infested with ghosts; they'll be invading the house next and we won't have a servant left on the place. Can't you do something to stop it?"

Radnor shrugged his shoulders and said that it was a pretty tough job to lay a ghost when there were twenty niggers on the place, but that he would see what he could do; and he presently drifted off again.

That same night about ten o'clock I was reading before going to bed, when a knock sounded on the door, and Radnor appeared. He was unusually restless and ill at ease. He referred in a jesting fashion to the ha'nt, discussed some neighborhood gossip, and finally quite abruptly inquired:

"Arnold, can you lend me some money?"

"Yes," I said, "I think so; how much do you want?"

"A hundred dollars if you can spare it. Fact is I'm a little hard up, and I've got a bill to meet. I have some money invested but I can't put my hands on it just this minute. I'll pay you in a week or so as soon as I get some cash—I wouldn't ask you, only my father is so blamed reluctant about paying my salary ahead of time."

I wrote out a check and handed it to him.

"Rad," I said, "you're perfectly welcome to the money; I'm glad to accommodate you, but if you'll excuse my mentioning it, I think you ought to pull up a bit on this poker business. You don't earn so much that if you're thinking of getting married you can afford to throw any of it away.—I'm only speaking for your good; it's no affair of mine," I added as I saw his face flush.

He hesitated a moment with the check in his hand; I know that he wanted to give it back, but he was evidently too hard pressed.

"Oh, keep the money!" I said. "I don't want to pry into your private affairs, only," I laughed, "I do want to see you win out ahead of Mattison, and I'm afraid you're not going about it the right way."

"Thank you, Arnold," he returned, "I want to win a great deal more than you want me to—and if it's gambling you're afraid of, you can ease your mind, for I've sworn off. It's not a poker debt I want this money for tonight; I wouldn't be so secretive about the business, only it concerns another person more than me."

"Radnor," I said, "I heard an ugly rumor the other day. I heard that the ghost was a live woman who was living in the deserted cabins under your connivance. I didn't believe it, but just the same it is not a story which you can afford to have even whispered."

Radnor raised his head sharply.

"Ah, I see!" His eyes wavered a moment and then fixed themselves miserably on my face. "Has—has Polly Mathers heard that?"

"Yes," I returned, "I fancy she has."

He struck the table with a quick flash of anger.

"It's a damned lie! And it comes from Jim Mattison."

And now as to the events which followed during the night. I've repeated them so many times to so many different persons that it is difficult for me to recall just what were my original sensations. I went to bed but I didn't go to sleep; this ha'nt business was getting on my nerves almost as badly as the Patterson-Pratt case. After a time I heard someone let himself softly out of the house; I knew well that it was Radnor and I didn't get up to look. I didn't want the appearance even to myself of spying upon him. After three quarters of an hour or so I was suddenly startled alert by hearing the squeak-squeak of a whippletree out on the lawn. It was the Colonel's buckboard which stood in need of oiling; I recognized the sound. Curiosity was too much for me this time. I slipped out of bed and hurried to the window. It was pretty dark outside, but there was a faint glimmer of starlight.

"Whoa, Jennie Loo; whoa!" I heard Rad's voice scarcely above a whisper, and I saw the outline of the cart plainly with Rad driving, and either some person or some large bundle on the seat beside him. It was on the side farthest from me, and was too vague to be distinguished. He made a wide detour of the house across the grass, and struck the driveway at the foot of the lawn; the reason for this manœuvre was evident—the gravel drive from the stables passed directly under the Colonel's window. I went back to bed half worried, half relieved. I strongly suspected that this was the end of the ghost; but I could not help puzzling over the part that Radnor had played in the little comedy—if comedy it were. The stories that I had heard about some of his disreputable associates returned to my mind with unpleasant emphasis.

I had gradually dozed off, when half waking, half sleeping, I heard the patter of bare feet on the veranda floor. The impression was not distinct enough to arouse me, and I have never been perfectly sure that I was not dreaming. I do not know how much time elapsed after this—I was sound asleep—when I was suddenly startled awake by a succession of the most horrible screams I have ever heard. In an instant I was on my feet in the middle of the floor. Striking a match and lighting a candle, I grabbed an umbrella—it was the only semblance of a weapon anywhere at hand—and dashed into the hall. The Colonel's door was flung open at the same instant, and he appeared on the threshold, revolver in hand.

"Eh, Arnold, what's happened?" he cried.

"I don't know," I gasped, "I'm going down to see."

We tumbled down stairs at such a rate that the candle went out, and we groped along in total darkness toward the rear of the house from where the sounds were coming. The cries had died down by this time into a horrible inarticulate wail, half animal, half human. I recognized the tones with a cold thrill; it was Mose. We found him groveling on the floor of the little passage that led from the dining-room to the serving room. I struck a light and we bent over him. I hated to look, expecting from the noise he was making to find him lying in a pool of blood. But he was entirely whole; there was no blood visible and we could find no broken bones. Apparently there was nothing the matter beyond fear, and of that he was nearly dead. He crawled to the Colonel and clung to his feet chattering an unintelligible gibberish. His eyes rolling wildly in the dim light, showed an uncanny yellow gleam. I could see where he got his name.

The Colonel's own nerves were beginning to assert themselves and with an oath he cuffed the fellow back to a state of coherence.

"Stand up, you blithering fool, and tell us what you mean by raising such a fuss."

Mose finally found his tongue but we still could make nothing of his story. He had been out "prospectin' 'round," and when he came in to go to bed—the house servants slept in a wing over the rear gallery—he met the ha'nt face to face standing in the dining-room doorway. He was so tall that his head reached the ceiling and he was so thin that you could see right through him. At the remembrance Mose began to shiver again. We propped him up with some whiskey and sent him off to bed still twittering with terror.

The Colonel was bent on routing out Radnor to share the excitement and I with some difficulty restrained him, knowing full well that Rad was not in the house. We made a search of the premises to assure ourselves that there was nothing tangible about Mose's ha'nt; but I was in such a hurry to get the Colonel safely upstairs again, that our search was somewhat cursory. We both overlooked the little office that opened off the dining-room. In spite of my manœuvres the Colonel entered the library first and discovered that the French window was open; he laid no stress on this however, supposing that Mose was the guilty one. He bolted it with unusual care, and I with equal care slipped back and unbolted it. I finally persuaded him that Mose's ha'nt was merely the result of a fevered imagination fed on a two weeks' diet of ghost stories, and succeeded in getting him back to bed without discovering Radnor's absence. I lay awake until I heard the sound of carriage wheels returning across the lawn, and, a few minutes later, footsteps enter the house and tip-toe upstairs. Then as daylight was beginning to show in the east I finally fell asleep, worn out with puzzling my head for an explanation which should cover at once Rad's nocturnal drive and Mose's ha'nt.

CHAPTER VI

WE SEND FOR A DETECTIVE

I slept late the next morning, and came down stairs to find the Colonel pacing the length of the dining-room, his head bent, a worried frown upon his brow. He came to a sudden halt at my appearance and regarded me a moment without speaking. I could see that something of moment had happened, but I could fathom nothing of its nature from his expression.

"Good morning, Arnold," he said with a certain grim pleasantness. "I have just been making a discovery. It appears that Mose's ha'nt amounted to more than we gave him credit for. The safe was robbed during the night."

"The safe robbed!" I cried. "How much was taken?"

"Something over a hundred dollars in cash, and a number of important papers."

He threw open the door of the little office, and waved his hand toward the safe which occupied one end. The two iron doors were wide open, the interior showing a succession of yawning pigeon holes with the cash drawer, half pulled out and empty. Several papers were spilled on the floor underneath.

"He evidently had no use for my will nor for Kennisburg street railway stock—I don't blame him; it wouldn't sell for the paper it's written on."

Radnor's step sounded on the stair as he came running down—whistling I noted.

"Ah—Rad," the Colonel called from the office doorway. "You're a good sleeper."

Radnor stopped his whistle as his eye fell upon our faces, and his own took on a look of anxiety.

"What's the matter?" he asked. "Has anything happened?"

"It appears the ha'nt has robbed the safe."

"The ha'nt?" Rad's face went visibly white, and then in a moment it cleared; his expression was divided between relief and dismay.

"Oh!" he said, "you've missed the money? I meant to get down first and tell you about it, but overslept. I took a hundred dollars out of the safe last night because I wanted the cash—you had gone to bed so I didn't say anything about it. I will ride into the village this morning and get it out of the bank in time to pay the men."

"You took a hundred dollars," the Colonel repeated. "And did you take the securities also and the bag of coin?" He waved his hand toward the safe. Radnor's eye followed and his jaw dropped.

"I didn't touch anything but the roll of bills in the cash drawer. What's missing?"

"Five thousand dollars in bonds, a couple of insurance policies and one or two deeds—also the bag of coin. Mose saw the ha'nt in the night, and Arnold and I came down to investigate; we unfortunately neglected the office in our search, or we might have cornered him. Do you happen to remember whether or not you closed the safe after you took out the money, and would you mind telling me why you needed a hundred dollars in such a hurry that you couldn't wait until the bank opened?"

The troubled line on Radnor's brow deepened.

"I think I closed the safe," he said, "but I don't remember. It's barely possible that I didn't lock it; you know we haven't always kept it locked, especially when there wasn't money in it.—It never occurred to me that anyone would steal the bonds. I can't imagine what it means."

"You haven't answered my question.—Why did you need a hundred dollars in cash after ten o'clock last night?"

"I am sorry, father, but I can't answer that question. It's a private matter."

"Indeed! You are sure that you did not take the bonds as well and have forgotten it?"

"I took one hundred dollars in bills and nothing else. I took that merely because it was my only way of cashing a check. I have frequently cashed my private checks, when we had a surplus on hand and I didn't want the bother of going in to the bank. So long as I balance the books all right, I see no reason why I should not do so."

"H'm!" said the Colonel. "Two days ago you came to me and wanted two months' pay in advance because you had overdrawn your bank account, and I refused to give it to you. Where, may I ask, were you intending to get the hundred dollars to pay back this amount?"

A quick flush spread over Radnor's face.

"I already had it—Arnold will tell you that, for I borrowed it of him."

"Certainly," I put in pacifically—"that's all settled between Rad and me. I have his note and was glad to accommodate him."

"Don't you get enough from me, that you must ask the guests in my house to supply you with money?"

Radnor's flush deepened but he said nothing. I could see by his eyes however that he would not stand much more.

"Then after you had helped yourself to the money, the bonds were stolen by someone else?" said the Colonel.

"So it appears," said Radnor.

"And have you any theory as to the identity of the thief?"

Rad hesitated a visible instant before replying. The flush left his face and the pallor came back, but in the end he raised his eyes and answered steadily.

"No, father, I have not. I am as much mystified as you are."

"And you heard nothing in the night? As I said before, you are an excellent sleeper!"

Rad caught an ironical undertone in his father's voice.

"I don't understand," he said.

"I am a trifle deaf myself, but still he wakened me.—It's strange that you should be the only one in the house who could sleep through it."

"Sleep through what? I don't know what you're talking about."

I cut in hastily and explained our adventure with Mose's ha'nt.

Radnor listened with troubled eyes but made no comment at the end. His father was watching him keenly, and I don't know whether it was intuition or some knowledge of the truth that made him suddenly put the question:

"You were of course in the house all night?"

"No," Radnor returned, "I was not. I didn't get in till early this morning and I suppose the excitement occurred during my absence."

"I suppose I may not be permitted to inquire where you spent the night—that too is a private matter?"

"Yes," said Radnor, easily, "that too is a private matter."

"And would throw no light on the robbery?"

"None whatever."

Solomon brought in the breakfast and we three sat down, but not to a very cheerful meal. The Colonel wore an angry frown and Rad an air of anxious perplexity. Neither of them indulged in any unnecessary conversation. I knew that the Colonel was more upset by his son's reticence than by the robbery of the bonds, and that it was my presence alone which restrained him from giving vent to his anger. As we rose from the table he said stiffly:

"Well, Rad, have you any suggestion as to how we shall set to work to track down the thief?"

Radnor slowly shook his head.

"I shall have to talk with Mose first and find out what he really saw."

"Mose!" The Colonel laughed shortly. "He's like all the rest of the niggers. He doesn't know what he saw—No sir! I've had enough of this ha'nt business; it's one thing when he spirits chickens from the oven, it's another when he takes to spiriting securities from the safe. I shall telegraph to Washington for a first class detective."

"If you take my advice," said Rad, "you'll not do that. A

detective's not much good outside the covers of a book. He'll stir up a lot of notoriety and present a bill; and you'll be no wiser than you were before."

"Whoever stole those bonds will be marketing them within a few days; the interest falls due the first of May. I am not so rich that I can let five thousand dollars go without a move to get it back. I shall telegraph today for a detective."

"Just as you please," said Radnor with a shrug, and he turned toward the door that opened on the gallery. Mose was visible at the end evidently recounting to an excited audience his experiences of the night. Rad beckoned to him and the two turned together across the lawn toward the laurel walk.

It was an hour or so later that Rad presented himself at my door. His colloquy with Mose had increased rather than lessened the mystified look on his face. He waited for no preliminaries this time, but plunged immediately into the matter that was on his mind.

"Arnold, for heaven's sake, stop my father from getting a detective down here. I don't dare say anything, for my opposition will only make him do it the more. But you have some influence with him; tell him you're a lawyer, and will take charge of it yourself."

"Why don't you want a detective?" I asked.

"Good Lord, hasn't our family had notoriety enough? Here's Nan eloping with the overseer, and Jeff the scandal of the county for five years. I can't turn around but some malicious interpretation is put on it, and now that the family ghost has taken to cracking safes gossip will never stop. Get a detective down here who goes nosing about the neighborhood in search of information and there's no telling where the thing will end. Those bonds can't be far. Aren't we more likely to get at the truth, if we lie low and don't let on we're after the thief?"

"Radnor," I said, "will you tell me the absolute truth? Have you any suspicion as to who took those securities? Do you know any facts which might lead to the apprehension of the thief?"

He remained silent a moment, then he parried my question with another.

"What time did all that row occur in the night?"

"I don't know; I didn't think to look, but I should say it was somewhere in the neighborhood of three o'clock. I didn't go to sleep again, and it was about half an hour later that you drove in."

"You heard me?"

"I heard you go and I heard you come; but I did not mention that fact to the Colonel."

Rad laughed shortly.

"I can at least prove an alibi," he said. "You can swear that I was not Mose's devil."

He remained silent a moment with his elbows on his knees and his chin in his hands studying the floor; then he raised his eyes to mine with a puzzled shake of the head.

"No, Arnold, I haven't the slightest suspicion as to who took those securities. I can't make it out. The robbery must have occurred while I was away. Of course the deeds and insurance policies and coin may have been taken as a blind; but it's queer. The money was in five and ten cent pieces and pennies—we always keep a lot of change on hand to pay the piece-workers during planting season. There was nearly a quart of it altogether and it must have weighed a ton. I can't imagine anyone stealing Government four-per-cents and pennies at the same haul."

"Did you get any light from Mose?" I asked.

"No, I can't make head nor tail out of his story. He isn't given to seeing visions, and as you know, he isn't afraid of the dark. He saw something that scared him; but what it was, I'll be darned if I know!"

"Then why not get a detective down and see if he can't find out?"

Radnor lowered his eyes a moment, then raised them frankly to mine.

"Oh, hang it, Arnold; I'm in the deuce of a hole! There's something else that I don't want found out. It's absolutely unconnected with the robbery, but you bring a detective down here and he's certain to stumble on that instead of the other. I'd tell you if I could, but really I can't just now. It's nothing I'm to blame for—my conduct lately has been immaculate. You get my father to abandon this detective plan, and we'll buckle down together and root out the truth about the robbery."

"Well," I promised, "I'll see what I can do; but as the Colonel says, five thousand dollars is a good deal of money to let slip through your hands without making an effort to get it back. You and I will have to finish the business if we undertake it."

"We will!" he assured me. "We can certainly get at the truth better than an outsider who doesn't know any of the facts. You switch off the old gentleman from putting it in the hands of the police and everything will come out right."

He went off actually whistling again. Whatever had been troubling him for the past two weeks had been sloughed off during the night, and all that remained now was the danger of detection; with this removed he was his old careless self. The loss of the securities was apparently not bothering him. Radnor always did exhibit a lordly disregard in money matters.

I lost no time in taking my errand to the Colonel, but I could discover him in none of the down stairs rooms nor anywhere else about the place. It occurred to me, after half an hour of searching, to see if his horse were in the stable; as I had surmised it was not. He had ordered it saddled immediately after breakfast and had ridden off in the direction of the village, one of the stable-men informed me. I had my own horse saddled, and ten minutes later was riding after him. It surprised me that he should have acted so quickly; the Colonel was usually rather given to procrastination, while Rad was the one who acted. His promptness proved that he was angry.

Four-Pools is about two miles from the village of Lambert Corners which consists of a single shady square. Two sides of the square are taken up with shops, the other two with the school, a couple of churches, and a dozen or so of dwellings. This composes as much of the town as is visible, the aristocracy being scattered over the outlying plantations, and regarding the "Corners" merely as a source of mail and drinks. Three miles farther down the pike lies Kennisburg, the county seat, which answers the varied purposes of a metropolis.

I reined in before "Miller's place," a spacious structure comprising a general store on the right, the post and telegraph office on the left, and in the rear a commodious room where a white man may quench his thirst. A negro must pass on to "Jake's place," two doors below. A number of horses were tied to the iron railing in front and among them I recognized Red Pepper. I found the Colonel in the back room, a glass of mint julep at his elbow, an interested audience before him. He was engaged in recounting the story of the missing bonds, and it was too late for me to interrupt. He referred in the most casual manner to the hundred dollars his son had taken from the safe the night before, a fortunate circumstance, he added, or that too would have been stolen. There was not the slightest suggestion in his tone that he and his son had had any words over this same hundred dollars. The Gaylord pride could be depended on for hiding from the world what the world had no business in knowing.

The telegram to the detective agency, I found, had already been dispatched, and the Colonel was awaiting his answer. It came in a few moments and was delivered by word of mouth, the clerk seeing no reason why he should put himself to the trouble of writing it out.

"They say they'll put one o' their best men on the case, Colonel, an' he'll get to the Junction at five-forty tonight."

The Colonel and I rode home together, he in a more placable frame of mind. Though I dare say he disliked as much as ever the idea of losing his bonds, still the éclat of a robbery, of a magnitude that demanded a detective, was something of a palliative. It was not everyone of his listeners who had five thousand dollars in bonds to lose. I knew that it would be useless to try to head off the detective now, and I wisely kept silent. My mind was by no means at rest however; for an unknown reason I did not want a detective any more than Radnor. I had the intangible feeling that there was something in the air which might better not be discovered.

CHAPTER VII

WE SEND HIM BACK AGAIN

The detective came. He was an inoffensive young man, and he set to work to unravel the mystery of the ha'nt with visible delight at the unusual nature of the job. Radnor received him in a spirit of almost anxious hospitality. A horse was given him to ride, guns and fishing tackle were placed at his disposal, a box of the Colonel's best cigars stood on the table of his room, and Solomon at his elbow presented a succession of ever freshly mixed mint juleps. I think that he was dazed and a trifle suspicious at these unexpected attentions; he was not used to the largeness of Southern hospitality. However, he set to work with an admirable zeal.

He interviewed the servants and farm-hands, and the information he received in regard to things supernatural would have filled three volumes; he was staggered by the amount of evidence at hand rather than the scarcity. He examined the safe and the library window with a microscope, crawled about the laurel walk on his hands and knees, sent off telegrams and gossiped with the loungers at "Miller's place." He interviewed the Colonel and Radnor, cross-examined me, and wrote down always copious notes. The young man's manner was preëminently professional.

Finally one evening—it was four days after his arrival—he joined me as I was strolling in the garden smoking an after dinner pipe.

"May I have just a word with you, Mr. Crosby?" he asked.

"I am at your service, Mr. Clancy," said I.

His manner was gravely portentous and prepared me for the statement that was coming.

"I have spotted my man," he said. "I know who stole the securities; but I am afraid that the information will not be welcome. Under the circumstances it seemed wisest to make my report to you rather than to Colonel Gaylord, and we can decide between us what is best to do."

"What do you mean?" I demanded. In spite of my effort at composure, there was anxiety in my tone.

"The thief is Radnor Gaylord."

I laughed.

"That is absolutely untenable. Rad is incapable of such an act in the first place, and in the second, he was not in the house when the robbery occurred."

"Ah! Then you know that? And where was he, pray?"

"That," said I, "is his own affair; if he did not tell you, it is because it is not connected with the case."

"So! It is just because it *is* connected with the case that he did not tell me. I will tell you, however, where he spent the night; he drove to Kennisburg—a larger town than Lambert Corners, where an unusual letter would create no comment—and mailed the bonds to a Washington firm of brokers with whom he has had some dealings. He took the bag of coin and several unimportant papers in order to deflect suspicion, and his opening the safe the night before for the hundred dollars was merely a ruse to allow him to forget and leave it open, so that the bonds could appear to be stolen by someone else. Just what led him to commit the act I won't say; he has been in a tight place for several months back in regard to money. Last January he turned a two-thousand dollar mortgage, that his father had given him on his twenty-first birthday, into cash, and what he did with the cash I haven't been able to discover. In any case his father knows nothing of the transaction; he thinks that Radnor still holds the mortgage. This spring the young man was hard up again, and no more mortgages left to sell. He probably did not regard the appropriation of the bonds as stealing, since everything by his father's will was to come to him ultimately.

"As to all this hocus-pocus about the ha'nt, that is easily explained. He needed a scapegoat on whom to turn the blame when the bonds should disappear; so he and this Cat-Eye Mose between them invented a ghost. The negro is a half crazy fellow who from the first has been young Gaylord's tool; I don't think he knew what he was doing sufficiently to be blamed. As for Gaylord himself, I fancy there was a third person somewhere in the background who was pressing him for money and who couldn't be shaken off till the money was forthcoming. But whatever his motive for taking the bonds, there is no doubt about the fact, and I have come to you with the story rather than to his father."

"It is absolutely impossible," I returned. "Radnor, whatever his faults, is an honorable man in regard to money matters. I have his word that he knows no more about the robbery of those bonds than I do."

The detective laughed.

"There is just one kind of evidence that doesn't count for much in my profession, and that is a man's word. We look for something a little more tangible—such as this for example."

He drew from his pocket an envelope, took from it a letter, and handed it to me. It was a typewritten communication from a firm of brokers in Washington.

> "Radnor F. Gaylord, Esq.,
> "Four-Pools Plantation, Lambert Corners, Va.
>
> "*Dear Mr. Gaylord*:
>
> "We are in receipt of your favor of April 29th. in regard to the sale of the bonds. The market is rather slow at present and we shall have to sell at 98¼. If you care to hold on to them a few months longer, there is every chance of the

market picking up, and we feel sure that in the end you will find them a good investment.

"Awaiting your further orders and thanking you for past favors,

"We are,

"Very truly yours,

"Jacoby, Haight & Co."

"Where did you get hold of that?" I asked. "It strikes me it's a private letter."

"Very private," the young man agreed. "I had trouble enough in getting hold of it; I had to do some fishing with a hook and pole over the transom of Mr. Gaylord's door. He had very kindly put the tackle at my disposal."

"You weren't called down here to open the family's private letters," I said hotly.

"I was called down here to find out who stole Colonel Gaylord's bonds, and I've done it."

I was silent for a moment. This letter from the brokers staggered me. April twenty-ninth was the date of the robbery, and I could think of no explanation. Clancy, noticing my silence, elaborated his theory with a growing air of triumph.

"This Mose was left behind the night of the robbery with orders to rouse the house while Radnor was away. Mose is a good actor and he fooled you. The obvious suspicion was that the ghost had stolen the bonds and you set out to find him—a somewhat difficult task as he existed only in Mose's imagination. I think when you reflect upon the evidence, you will see that my explanation is convincing."

"It isn't in the least convincing," I retorted. "Mose was not acting; he saw something that frightened him half out of his senses. And that something was not Radnor masquerading as a ghost, for Radnor was out of the house when the robbery took place."

"Not necessarily. The robbery took place early in the evening before all this rumpus occurred. Even if Mose did see a ghost, the ghost had nothing to do with it."

"You have absolutely no proof of that; it is nothing but surmise."

Clancy smiled with an air of patient tolerance.

"How about the letter?" he inquired. "How do you explain that?"

"I don't explain it; it is none of my business. But I dare say Radnor will do so readily enough—there he is going toward the stables; we will call him over."

"No, hold on, I haven't finished what I want to say. I was employed by Colonel Gaylord to find out who stole the bonds and I have done so. But the Colonel did not suspect the direction my investigations would take or he never would have engaged me. Now I am wondering if it would not be kinder not to let him know? He's had trouble enough with his elder son; Radnor is all he has left. The young man seems to me like a really decent fellow—I dare say he'll straighten up and amount to something yet. Probably he considered the money as practically his already; anyway he's been decent to me and I should like to do him a service. Now say we three talk it over together and settle it out of court as it were. I've put in my time down here and I've got to have my pay, but perhaps it would be better all around if I took it from the young man rather than his father."

This struck me as the best way out of the muddle, and a very fair proposition, considering Clancy's point of view. I myself did not for an instant credit his suspicions, but I thought the wisest thing to do was to tell Rad just how the matter stood and let him explain in regard to the letter. I left Clancy waiting in the summer house while I went in search of Rad. I wished to be the one to do the explaining as I knew he was not likely to take any such accusation calmly.

I found him in the stables, and putting my hand on his shoulder, marched him back toward the garden.

"Rad," I said, "Clancy has formed his conclusions as to how the bonds left the safe, and I want you to convince him that he is mistaken."

"Well? Let's hear his conclusions."

"He thinks that you took them when you took the money."

"You mean that I stole them?"

"That's what he thinks."

"He does, does he? Well he can prove it!"

Radnor broke away from me and strode toward the summer house. The detective received his onslaught placidly; his manner suggested that he was used to dealing with excitable young men.

"Sit down, Mr. Gaylord, and let's discuss this matter quietly. If you listen to reason, I assure you it will go no further."

"Do you mean to say that you accuse me of stealing those bonds?" Radnor shouted.

Clancy held up a warning hand.

"Don't talk so loud; someone will hear you. Sit down." He nodded toward a seat on the other side of the little rustic table. "I will explain the matter as I see it, and if you can disprove any of my statements I shall be more than glad to have you."

Radnor subsided and listened scowlingly while the detective outlined his theory in a perfectly non-personal way, and ended by producing the letter.

"Where did you get that?" Rad demanded.

"Out of your coat pocket which I hooked over the transom of the door." He made the statement imperturbably; it was evidently a matter of everyday routine.

"So you enter gentlemen's houses as their guest and spend your time sneaking about reading their private correspondence?"

An angry gleam appeared in Clancy's eye and he rose to his feet.

"I did not come to your house as your guest. I came on business for Colonel Gaylord. Now that my business is completed I will make my report to him and go."

Radnor rose also.

"It's a lie, and you haven't a word of proof to show."

Clancy significantly tapped the pocket that held the letter.

"That," said Radnor contemptuously, "refers to two bonds which I bought last winter with some money I got from selling a mortgage. I preferred to have the investment in bonds because they are more readily negotiable. I left them at my broker's as collateral for another investment I was making. Last week I needed some ready money and wrote to them to sell. My statement can easily be substantiated; no reputable detective would ever base any such absurd charge on the contents of a letter he did not understand."

"Of course," said the detective, "we have tried to get at the matter from the other end; but Jacoby, Haight & Company refuse to discuss the affairs of their clients. I did not press the point as I did not want to stir up comment. However," he smiled, "I must confess, Mr. Gaylord, that I think your explanation a trifle fishy. Perhaps you will answer one question. Did you mail your letter to them in Kennisburg the night of the robbery with a special delivery stamp?"

"It happens that I did, but it was merely a coincidence and has nothing to do with the robbery."

"Will you be kind enough to explain why you drove to Kennisburg in the night and why you needed the money so suddenly?"

"No, I will not. That is a matter which concerns, me alone."

"Very well! As it happens I do not base my charge on the letter; I had already formed my opinion before I knew of its existence. Do you deny that you yourself have encouraged the belief in the ghost among the negroes? That on more than one occasion, you, or your accomplice, Cat-Eye Mose, have masqueraded as the ghost? That, while you were pretending to Colonel Gaylord to be as much puzzled by the matter as he, you were in truth at the bottom of the whole business?"

Radnor glanced uneasily at me and hesitated before replying.

"No," he said at length, "I don't deny that, but I do affirm that it has nothing to do with the robbery."

The detective laughed.

"You must excuse me, Mr. Gaylord, if I stick to the opinion that I have solved the puzzle."

He turned with a motion toward the house, and Radnor barred the entrance.

"Do you think I lie when I say I know nothing of those bonds?"

"Yes, Mr. Gaylord, I do."

For a moment I thought that Radnor was going to strike him, but I pulled him back and turned to Clancy.

"He knows nothing about the bonds," said I, "but nevertheless you must not take any such story to Colonel Gaylord. He is an old man, and while he would not believe his son guilty of theft, still it would worry him. There is something else that happened that night—entirely uncriminal—but which we do not wish him to hear about. Therefore I am not going to let you go to him with this nonsensical tale that you have cooked up."

This was a trial shot on my part but it hit the bull's-eye. Radnor stared but said nothing; and the detective visibly wavered.

"Now," I added, taking out my checkbook, "suppose I pay you what you would have received had you discovered the bonds, and dispense with your further services?"

"That's just as you say. I feel that I've done the job and am entitled to the money. If you wish to pay it, all right; otherwise I get it from Colonel Gaylord. I received a retaining fee and was to have two hundred dollars more when I located the bonds. In order not to stir up any bad feeling I'm willing to take that two hundred dollars from you and drop the matter."

"It's blackmail!" said Radnor.

"Keep still, Rad," I said. "It's very accommodating of Mr. Clancy to see it this way."

I wrote out a check and tossed it to the detective.

"Now go to Colonel Gaylord," I said, "tell him that you have been unsuccessful in finding any clue; that the bonds will almost certainly be marketed in the city, and that your only hope of tracing them is to work from the other end. Then pack your bag and go. A carriage will be ready to take you to the Junction in half an hour."

"Just wait a moment, Mr. Clancy," Rad called after him as he turned away. He drew a note book from his pocket and ripping out a page scrawled across the face:

> "Jacoby, Haight and Co.
>
> "*Gentlemen*:—You will oblige me by answering any questions which the bearer of this note may ask concerning my past transactions with you.
>
> "Radnor F. Gaylord."

"There," said Rad, thrusting it toward him, "kindly make use of that when you get to Washington, and in the future I should advise you to base your charges on something a little more substantial."

His manner was insultingly contemptuous, but Clancy swallowed it with smiling good nature.

"I shall be interested in continuing the investigation," he observed as he pocketed the paper and withdrew.

CHAPTER VIII

THE ROBBERY REMAINS A MYSTERY

So we got rid of the detective. But matters did not readily settle down again into their old relations. The Colonel was irritable, and Rad was moody and sullen. He showed no tendency to confide in me as to the truth about the ha'nt, and I did not probe the matter further. In a day or so he brought me three hundred dollars, to cover the amount I had loaned him, together with the "blackmail," as he insisted upon calling it. The money, he informed me, was from the proceeds of the bonds he had sold. He showed me at the same time several letters from his brokers establishing beyond a doubt that the story he had told was true. As to the stolen bonds, their whereabouts was as much a mystery as ever, and Rad appeared to take not the slightest interest in the matter. Since the detective had been summoned, he had washed his hands of all responsibility.

I think it was the morning after Clancy's departure that Solomon handed me a pale blue envelope bearing in the upper left-hand corner the device of the Post-Dispatch. I laughed as I ripped it open; I had almost forgotten Terry's existence. It contained a characteristic pencil scrawl slanting across a sheet of yellow copy paper.

"Arnold Crosby, Esq.,
"Turnips Farm, Pumpkin Corners, Va.

"*Dear Sir*:

"Enclosed please find clipping. Are the facts straight and have the missing bonds turned up? If not, don't you want me to run down and find them for you? Should like to meet an authenticated ghost. Wouldn't be a bad Sunday feature article. Give it my love. Is it a man or lady? Things are also moving nicely in New York—two murders and a child abducted in one week.

"How are crops?

"Yours truly,

"T. P.

"Wire me if you want me."

The clipping was headed, "Spook Cracks Safe," and was a fairly accurate account of the ha'nt and the robbery. It ended with the remark that the mystery was as yet unsolved, but that the best detective talent in the country had been engaged on the case.

I tossed the letter to Radnor with a laugh; he had already heard of Terry's connection with the Patterson-Pratt affair.

"Perhaps we couldn't do better than to get him down," I suggested; "he's most abnormally keen at ferreting out a mystery that promises any news—if any one can learn the truth about those bonds, he can."

"I don't want to know the truth," Radnor growled. "I'm sick of the very name of bonds."

And this had been his attitude from the moment the detective left. My own insistence that it was our duty to track down the thief met with nothing but a shrug. Another person might have suspected that this apathy only proved his own culpability in the theft, but such a suspicion never for a moment crossed my mind. He was, as he said, sick of the very name of bonds, and with a person of his temperament that ended the matter. Though I did not comprehend his attitude, still I took him at his word. There was something about Rad's straightforward way of looking one in the eye that impelled belief. As I had heard the Colonel boast, a Gaylord could not tell a lie.

The things a Gaylord could and could not do, were, I acknowledge, to a Northern ethical sense a trifle mystifying. A Gaylord might drink and gamble and fail to pay his debts (not his gambling debts; his tailor and his grocer); he might be the hero of many doubtful affairs with women; he might in a sudden fit of passion commit a murder—there was more than one killing in the family annals—but under no circumstances would his "honah" permit him to tell a lie. The reservation struck me somewhat humorously as an anti-climax. But nevertheless I believed it. When Rad said he knew nothing of the stolen bonds I dismissed the possibility from my mind.

Though I was relieved to feel that he was not guilty, still I was worried and nervous over the matter. I felt that it was criminal not to do something, and yet my hands were tied. I could scarcely undertake an investigation myself, for every clue led across the trail of the ha'nt, and that, Rad made it clear, was forbidden ground. The Colonel, meanwhile, was comparatively quiet, as he supposed the detective was still working on the case. I accordingly did nothing, but I kept my eyes open, hoping that something would turn up.

Rad's temper was absolutely unbearable for the first week after the detective left. The reason had nothing to do with the stolen bonds, but was concerned entirely with Polly Mathers's behavior. She barely noticed Rad's existence, so occupied was she with the ecstatic young sheriff. What the trouble was, I did not know, but I suspected that it was the whispered conjectures in regard to the ha'nt.

I remember one evening in particular that she snubbed him in the face of the entire neighborhood. We had arrived at a party a trifle late to find Polly as usual the center of a laughing group of young men, all clamoring for dances. They widened their circle to admit Rad in a way which tacitly acknowledged his prior claim. He inquired with his most deferential bow what dances she had saved for him. Polly replied in an off-hand manner that she was sorry but her card was already full. Rad shrugged nonchalantly, and sauntering toward the door, disappeared for the rest of the night. When he turned up at Four-Pools early in the morning, his horse, Uncle Jake informed me, looked as if it had been ridden by "de debbil hisself."

With Radnor in this state, and the Colonel growing daily more irritable over the continued mystery of the bonds, it is not strange that matters between them were at a high state of tension. As I saw more of the Colonel's treatment of Rad, I came to realize that there was considerable excuse for Jefferson's wildness. While he was a kind man at heart, still he had an ungovernable temper, and an absolutely tyrannical desire to rule every one about him. His was the only free will allowed on the place. He attempted to treat Rad at twenty-two much as he had done at twelve. A few months before my arrival (I heard this later) he had even struck him, whereupon Radnor had turned on his heel and walked out of the house, and had only consented to come back two weeks later when he heard that the old man was ill. If two men ever needed a woman to manage them, these were the two. I think that if my aunt had lived, most of the trouble would have been avoided.

Rad was not the only one, however, who felt the Colonel's irritation over the robbery. His treatment of the servants was harsh and even cruel. Everybody on the place went about in a half-cowed fashion. He treated Mose like a dog. Why the fellow stood it, I don't know. The Colonel seemed never to have learned that the old slave days were over and that he no longer owned the negroes body and soul. His government of the plantation was in the manner of a despot. Everybody—from his own son to the merest pickaninny—was at the mercy of his caprice. When he was in good humor, he was kindness itself to the darkies; when he was in bad humor, he vented his anger on whoever happened to be nearest.

I shall never forget the feeling of indignation with which I first saw him strike a man. A strange negro was caught one morning in the neighborhood of the chicken coop, and was brought up to the house by two of the stable-men. My uncle, who was standing on the portico steps waiting for his horse, was in a particularly savage mood, as he had just come from an altercation with Radnor. The man said that he was hungry and asked for work. But the Colonel, almost without waiting to hear him speak, fell upon him in a fit of blind rage, slashing him half a dozen times over the head and shoulders with his heavy riding crop. The negro, who was a powerfully built fellow, instead of standing up and defending himself like a man, crouched on the ground with his arms over his head.

"Please, Cunnel Gaylord," he whimpered, "le' me go! I ain't done nuffen. I ain't steal no chickens. For Gord's sake, doan whip me!"

I sprang forward with an angry exclamation and grasped my uncle's arm. The fellow was on his feet instantly and off down the lane without once glancing back. The Colonel stood a moment looking from my indignant face to the man disappearing in the distance, and burst out laughing.

"I reckon I won't be troubled with *him* any more," he remarked as he mounted and rode away, his good humor apparently quite restored.

I confess that it took me some time to get over that scene. But the worst of it was that he treated his own servants in the same summary fashion. The thing that puzzled me most was the way in which they received it. Mose, being always at hand, was cuffed about more than any negro on the place, but as far as I could make out, it only seemed to increase his love and veneration for the Colonel. I don't believe the situation could ever be intelligible to a Northern man.

So matters stood when I had been a month at Four-Pools. My vacation had lasted long enough, but I was supremely comfortable and very loath to go. The first few weeks of May had been, to my starved city eyes, a dazzling pageant of beauty. The landscape glowed with yellow daffodils, pink peach blossoms, and the bright green of new wheat; the fields were alive with the frisky joyousness of spring lambs and colts, turned out to pasture. It was with a keen feeling of reluctance that I faced the prospect of New York's brick and stone and asphalt. My work was calling, but I lazily postponed my departure from day to day.

Things at the plantation seemed to have settled into their old routine. The whereabouts of the bonds was still a mystery, but the ha'nt had returned to his grave—at least, in so far as any manifestations affected the house. I believe that the "sperrit of de spring-hole" had been seen rising once or twice from a cloud of sulphurous smoke, but the excitement was confined strictly to the negro quarters. No man on the place who valued a whole skin would have dared mention the word "ha'nt" in Colonel Gaylord's presence. Relations between Rad and his father were rather less strained, and matters on the whole were going pleasantly enough, when there suddenly fell from a clear sky the strange and terrible series of events which changed everything at Four-Pools.

CHAPTER IX

THE EXPEDITION TO LURAY

Toward eleven o'clock one morning, the Colonel, Radnor and I were established in lounging chairs in the shade of a big catalpa tree on the lawn. It was a warm day, and Rad and I were just back from a tramp to the upper pasture—a full mile from the house. We were addressing ourselves with considerable zest to the frosted glasses that Solomon had just placed on the table, when we became aware of the sound of galloping hoofs, and a moment later Polly Mathers and her sorrel mare, Tiger Lilly, appeared at the end of the sunflecked lane. An Irish setter romped at her side, and the three of them made a picture. The horse's shining coat, the dog's silky hair and Polly's own red gold curls were almost of a color. I believe the little witch had chosen the two on purpose. In her dark habit and mannish hat, with sparkling cheeks and laughing eyes, she was as pretty an apparition as ever enhanced a May morning. She waved her crop gaily and rode toward us across the lawn.

"Howdy!" she called, in a droll imitation of the mountain dialect. "Ain't you-uns guine to ask me to 'light a while, an' set a bit, an' talk a spell?"

Radnor's face had flushed quickly as he perceived who the rider was, but he held himself stiffly in the background while the Colonel and I did the honors. It was the first time, I know, that Polly and Rad had met since the night she refused to dance with him; and her appearance could only be interpreted as a desire to make amends.

She sprang lightly to the ground, turned Tiger Lilly loose to graze about the lawn, and airily perched herself on the arm of a chair. There was nothing in her manner, at least, to suggest that her relations with any one of us were strained. After a few moments of neighborly gossip with the Colonel and me—Rad was monosyllabic and remote—she arrived at her errand. Some friends from Savannah were stopping at the Hall on their way to the Virginia hot springs, and, as is usual, when strangers visit the valley, they were planning an expedition to Luray Cave. The cave was on the other side of the mountains about ten miles from Four-Pools. Since I had not yet visited it (that was at least the reason she gave) she had come to ask the three of us to join the party on the following day.

Rad was sulky at first, and rather curtly declined on the ground that he had to attend to some business. But Polly scouted his excuse, and added significantly that Jim Mattison had not been asked. He accepted this mark of repentance with a pleased flush, and before she rode away, he had become his former cheerful self again. The Colonel also demurred on the ground that he was getting too old for such diversions, but Polly laid her hands upon his shoulders and coaxed him into acquiescence—even a mummy must have unbent before such persuasion. As a matter of fact though, the Colonel was only too pleased with his invitation. It flattered him to be included with the young people, and he was immensely fond of Polly.

It struck me suddenly as I watched her, how like she was to that other girl, of eighteen years before. There danced in Polly's eyes the same eager joy of life that vitalized the face of the portrait over the mantelpiece upstairs. The resemblance for a moment was almost startling; I believe the same thought had come to Colonel Gaylord. The old man's eyes dwelt upon her with a sadly wistful air; and I like to feel that it was of Nannie he was thinking.

Radnor and I had been invited to a dance that same evening at a neighboring country house, but when the time came, I begged off on the plea of wishing to rest for the ride the next morning.

The real reason, I fancy, was that I too was suffering from a touch of Radnor's trouble; and, since I had no chance of winning her, it was the part of wisdom to keep out of hearing of Polly's laugh. In any case, I went to bed and to sleep, while Rad went to the party, and I have never known exactly what happened that night.

I rose early the next morning, and as I went down stairs I saw Solomon crawling around on his hands and knees on the parlor floor, collecting the remnants of a French clock which had stood on the mantelpiece.

"How did that clock come to be broken?" I asked a trifle sharply, thinking I had caught him in a bad piece of carelessness.

"Cayn't say, sah," Solomon returned, rising on his knees and looking at me mournfully. "I specs ole Marsa been chastisin' young Marsa again. It's powe'ful destructive on de brick-yuh-brack."

I went on out of doors, wondering sadly if Radnor could have been drinking, and accusing myself for not having gone to the party and kept him straight. It was evident at breakfast that something serious had happened between him and his father. The Colonel appeared unusually grave, and Rad, after a gruff "good morning," sat staring at his plate in a dogged silence. Throughout the meal he scarcely so much as exchanged a glance with his father. I tried to talk as if I noticed nothing; and in the course of the somewhat one-sided conversation, happened to mention our proposed trip to Luray. Rad returned that he had visited the cave a good many times and did not care about going. I was puzzled at this, for I knew that the cave was not the chief attraction, but I discreetly dropped the subject and shortly after we rose from the table.

As I left the room I saw the Colonel walk over and lay his hand on Radnor's arm.

"You will change your mind and go, my boy," he said.

But Rad shook the hand off roughly and turned away. As I went on out to the stables to give orders about the horses, I felt in anything but the proper spirits for a day of merry-making. However much the Colonel may have been to blame in their quarrel of the night before—and the French clock told its own story—still I could not help but feel that Rad should have borne with him more patiently. The scene I had just witnessed in the dining-room made me miserable. The Colonel was a proud man and apology came hard for him, his son might at least have met him half way.

Going upstairs to my room a few minutes later, I caught a glimpse through the open door, of someone standing before the mantelpiece. Thinking it was Radnor waiting to consult me, I hurried forward and reached the threshold before I realized that it was the Colonel. He was standing with folded arms before the picture, his eyes, gleaming from under beetling brows, were devouring it hungrily, line by line. His face was set rigidly with a look—whether of sorrow or loneliness or remorse, I do not know; but I do know that it was the saddest expression I have ever seen on any human face. It was as if, in a single illuminating flash, he had looked into his own soul, and seen the ruin that his ungoverned pride and passion had wrought against those he loved the most.

So absorbed had he been with his thoughts, that he had not heard my step. I turned and stole away, realizing suddenly that he was an old man, broken, infirm; that his life with its influence for good or evil was already at an end; he could never change his character now, no matter how keenly he might realize his defects. Poor little Nannie's wilfulness was at last forgiven, but the forgiveness was fifteen years too late. Why could not that moment of insight have come earlier to Colonel Gaylord, have come in time to save him from his mistakes?

I passed out of doors again, pondering somewhat bitterly the exigencies of human life. The bright spring morning with its promise of youth and joy seemed jarringly out of tune. The beauty was but surface deep, I told myself pessimistically; underneath it was a cruel world. Before me in the garden path, a jubilant robin was pulling an unhappy angle worm from the ground, and a little farther on, under a blossoming apple tree, the kitchen cat was breakfasting on a baby robin. The double spectacle struck me as significant of life. I was casting about for some philosophical truths to fit it, when my revery was interrupted by a shout from Radnor.

I turned to find the horses—three of them—waiting at the portico steps. Rad was going then after all. He and his father had evidently patched up some sort of a truce, but I soon saw that it was only a truce. The two avoided crossing eyes, and as we rode along they talked to me instead of to each other.

The party met at Mathers Hall. The plan was for us to ride to Luray that morning, spend most of the afternoon there, and then return to the Hall for a supper and dance in the evening. The elder ladies took the carriage, while the rest of us went on horseback, a couple of servants following in the buckboard with the luncheon. Mose, bare-feet, linsey-woolsey and all, was brought along to act as guide and he was fairly purring with contentment at the importance it gave him over the other negroes. It seems that he had been in the habit of finding his way around in the cave ever since he was a little shaver, and he knew the route, Radnor told me, better than the professional guides. He knew it so well, in fact, that the entire neighborhood was in the habit of borrowing him whenever expeditions were being planned to Luray.

We left our horses at the village hotel, and after eating a picnic lunch in the woods, set out to make the usual round of the cave. Luray has since been lighted with electricity and laid out in cement walks, but the time of which I am writing was before its exploitation by the railroad, and the cavern was still in its natural state. Each of us carried either candles or a torch, and the guides were supplied with calcium lights which they touched off at intervals whenever there was any special object of interest. This was the first cavern of any size that I had ever visited and I was so taken up with examining the rock formations and keeping my torch from burning my hands that I did not pay much attention to the disposal of the rest of the party. It took over two hours to make the round, and we must have walked about five miles.

What with the heavy damp air and the slippery path, I, for one, was glad to get out into the sunshine again.

I joined the group about Polly Mathers and casually asked if she knew where Radnor had gone.

"I haven't seen him for some time; I think he must have come out before us," she replied. "And unless I am mistaken, Colonel Gaylord," she added, turning to my uncle, "he left my coat on that broken column above Crystal Lake. I am afraid that he isn't a very good cavalier."

The Colonel, I imagine, had been a very good cavalier in his own youth, and I do not think that he had entirely outgrown it.

"I will repair his fault, Miss Polly," the old man returned with a courtly bow, "and prove to you that the boy does not take after his father in lack of gallantry."

"No, indeed, Colonel Gaylord!" Polly exclaimed. "I was only joking; I shouldn't think of letting you go back after it. One of the servants can get it."

I shortly after ran across Mose and sent him back for the coat, and the incident was forgotten. We straggled back to the hotel in twos and threes; the horses were brought out, and we got off amidst general confusion.

I rode beside the carriage for a couple of miles exchanging courtesies with Mrs. Mathers, and then galloped ahead to join the other riders. I was surprised to see neither my uncle nor Radnor anywhere in sight, and inquired as to their whereabouts.

"I thought they were riding with you," said Polly, wheeling to my side. "You don't suppose," she asked quickly, "that the Colonel was foolish enough to go back for my coat, and we've left him behind?"

One of the men laughed.

"He has a horse, Miss Polly, and he knows how to use it. I dare say, even if we did leave him behind, that he can find his way home."

"I sent Mose back for the coat," I remarked. "The Colonel probably feels that he has had enough frivolity for one day, and has preferred to ride straight on to Four-Pools."

It occurred to me that Rad and his father had ridden home together to make up their quarrel, and the reflection added considerably to my peace of mind. I had felt vaguely uncomfortable over the matter all day, for I knew that the old man was always miserable after a misunderstanding with his son, and I strongly suspected that Radnor himself was far from happy.

When we arrived at Mathers Hall, Polly slipped from her saddle and came running up to me as I was about to dismount. She laid her hand on the bridle and asked, in the sweetest way possible, if I would mind riding back to the plantation to see if the Colonel were really there, as she could not help feeling anxious about him. I noticed with a smile that she made no comment on the younger man's defection, though I strongly suspected that she was no less interested in that. I turned about and galloped off again, willing enough to do her bidding, though I could not help reflecting that it would have been just as easy for her, and considerably easier for me, had she developed her anxiety a few miles back.

When I reached the four corners where the road to Four-Pools branches off from the valley turnpike, I saw the wagon coming with the two Mathers negroes in it, but without any sign of Mose. I drew up and waited for them.

"Hello, boys!" I called. "What's become of Mose?"

"Dat's moh 'n I can say, Mista Ahnold," one of the men returned. "We waited foh him a powe'ful while, but it 'pears like he's 'vaporated. I reckon he's took to de woods an' is gwine to walk home. Dat Cat-Eye Mose, he's monstrous fond ob walkin'!"

I do not know why this incident should have aroused my own anxiety, but I pushed on to the plantation with a growing feeling of uneasiness. Nothing had been seen of either the Colonel or Mose, Solomon informed me, but he added with an excited rolling of his eyes:

"Marse Rad, he come back nearly an hour ago an' stomp roun' like he mos' crazy, an' den went out to de gahden."

I followed him and found him sitting in the summer house with his elbows on his knees and his head in his hands.

"What's the matter, Rad?" I cried in alarm. "Has anything happened to your father?"

He looked up with a start at the sound of my voice, and I saw that his face was pale.

"My father?" he asked in a dazed way. "I left him in the cave. Why do you ask?"

"He didn't come back with the rest of us, and Polly asked me to find him."

"He's old enough to take care of himself," said Radnor without looking up.

I hesitated a moment, uncertain what to do, and then turned back to the stables to order a fresh horse. To my astonishment I found the stable-men gathered in a group about Rad's mare, Jennie Loo. She was dashed with foam and trembling, and appeared to be about used up. The men fell back and eyed me silently as I approached.

"What's happened to the horse?" I cried. "Did she run away?"

One of the men "reckoned" that "Marse Rad" had been whipping her.

"Whipping her!" I exclaimed in dismay. It was unbelievable, for no one as a rule was kinder to animals than Radnor; and as for his own Jennie Loo, he couldn't have cared more for her if she had been a human being. There was no mistaking it however. She was crossed and recrossed with thick welts about the withers; it was evident that the poor beast had been disgracefully handled.

Uncle Jake volunteered that Rad had galloped straight into the stable, had dropped the bridle and walked off without a word; and he added the opinion that a "debbil had done conjured him." I was inclined to agree. There seemed to be something in the air that I did not understand, and my anxiety for the Colonel suddenly rushed back fourfold. I wheeled about and ordered a horse in an unnecessarily sharp tone, and the men jumped to obey me.

It was just sunset as I mounted again and galloped down

the lane. For the second time that day I set out along the lonely mountain road leading to Luray, but this time with a vague fear gripping at my heart. Why had Radnor acted so strangely, I asked myself again and again. Could it be connected with last night's quarrel? And where was the Colonel, and where was Mose?

CHAPTER X

THE TRAGEDY OF THE CAVE

It was almost dark by the time I reached the village of Luray. I galloped up to the hotel where we had left our horses that morning and without dismounting called out to the loafers on the veranda to ask if anyone had seen Colonel Gaylord. Two or three of them, glad of a diversion, got up and sauntered out to the stepping-stone where I waited, to discuss the situation.

What was the matter? they inquired. Hadn't the Colonel gone home with the rest of the party?

No, he had not, I returned impatiently, and I wanted to know if any of them had seen him.

They consulted together and finally decided that no one had seen him, and at this the stable boy vouchsafed the information that Red Pepper was still in the barn.

"I thought maybe the Colonel was intending to make me a present of that horse," the landlord observed with a grin, as he joined the group.

A chuckle ran around the circle at this sally. It was evident that the Colonel did not have a reputation in the county for making presents. I impatiently gathered up my reins and one of the men remarked:

"I reckon young Gaylord got home in good time. He was in an almighty hurry when he started. He didn't stop for no farewells."

With numerous interruptions and humorous interpolations, they finally managed to tell me in their exasperatingly slow drawl that Rad had come back to the hotel that afternoon before the rest of the party, had drunk two glasses of brandy, called for his horse, and galloped off without speaking a word to anyone except to swear at the stable boy. The speaker finished with the assertion that in his opinion Rad Gaylord and Jeff Gaylord were cut out of the same block.

I shifted my seat uneasily. This information did not tend to throw any light on the question of the Colonel's whereabouts, and I was in no mood just then to listen to any more gossip about Rad.

"I'm not looking for young Gaylord," I said shortly. "I know where he is. It's the Colonel I'm after. Neither he nor Cat-Eye Mose have come back, and I'm afraid they're lost in the cave."

The men laughed at this. People didn't get lost in the cave, they said. All anyone had to do was to follow the path; and besides, if the Colonel was with Mose he couldn't get lost if he tried. Mose knew the cave so well that he could find his way around it in the dark. Colonel Gaylord had probably met some friends in the village and driven home with them.

But I would not be satisfied with an explanation of that sort. The Colonel, I knew, was not in the habit of abandoning horses in any such casual manner; and even supposing he had gone home with some friends, he would scarcely have taken Mose along.

I dismounted, turned my horse over to the stable boy, and announced that the cave must be searched. This request was received with some amusement. The idea of getting out a search party for Cat-Eye Mose struck them as peculiarly ludicrous. But I insisted, and finally one of the men who was in the habit of acting as guide, took his feet down from the veranda railing with a grunt of disapproval and shambled into the house after some candles and a lantern. Two or three of the others joined the expedition after a good deal of chaffing at my expense.

We set out for the mouth of the cave by a short cut that led across the fields. It was quite dark by this time, and as there was no moon our one lantern did not go far toward lighting the path. We stumbled along over plowed ground and through swampy pastures to the music of croaking frogs and whip-poor-wills. At first the way was enlivened by humorous suggestions on the part of my companions as to what had become of Colonel Gaylord, but as I did not respond very freely to their bantering, they finally fell silent with only an occasional imprecation as someone stubbed his toe or caught his clothing on a brier. After a half hour or so of plodding we came to a clear path through the woods and in a few minutes reached the mouth of the cave.

A rough little shanty was built over the entrance. It was closed by a ramshackle door which a child could have opened without any difficulty; there was at least no danger of the Colonel's having been locked inside. Lighting our candles, we descended the rough stone staircase into the first great vault, which forms a sort of vestibule to the caverns. With our hands to our mouths we hallooed several times and then held our breath while we waited for an answer. The only sound which came out of the stillness was the occasional drip of water or the flap of a bat's wing. Had the Colonel been lost in any of the winding passages he must have heard us and replied, for the slightest sound is audible in such a cavern, echoing and re-echoing as it does through countless vaulted galleries. The silence, however, instead of assuring me that he was not there only increased my uneasiness. What if he had slipped on the wet clay, and having injured himself, was lying unconscious in the darkness?

The men wished to turn back, but I insisted that we go as far as the broken column which lies in a little gallery above Crystal Lake. That was the place where the coat had been left, and we could at least find out if either the Colonel or Mose had returned for it. We set out in single file along the damp clay path, the light from our few candles only serving to intensify the blackness around us. The huge white forms of the stalactites seemed to follow us like ghosts in the gloom; every now and then a bat flapped past our faces, and I wondered with a shiver how anyone could get up courage to go alone into such a hole as that.

"Crystal Lake" is a shallow pool lying in a sort of bowl. On the farther side the path runs up seven or eight feet above the water along the broken edge of a cliff. A few steps beyond the pool the path diverges sharply to the left and opens into the little gallery of the broken column.

Just as we were about to ascend the two or three stone steps leading to the incline, the guide in front stopped short, and clutching me by the arm pointed a shaking forefinger toward the pool.

"What's that?" he gasped.

I strained my eyes into the darkness but I could see nothing.

"There, that black thing under the bank," he said, raising his candle and throwing the light over the water.

We all saw it now and recognized it with a thrill of horror. It was the body of Colonel Gaylord. He was lying on his face at the bottom of the pool, and with outstretched arms was clutching the mud in his hands. The still water above him was as clear as crystal but was tinged with red.

"It's my uncle!" I cried, springing forward. "He's fallen over the bank. He may not be dead."

But they held me back.

"He's as dead as he ever will be," the guide said grimly. "An' what's more, Colonel Gaylord warn't the man to drown in three foot o' water without making a struggle. This ain't no accident. It's murder! We must go back an' get the coroner. It's agen the law to touch the body until he comes."

It went to my heart to leave the old man lying there at the bottom of that pool, but I could not prevail on one of them to help me move him. The coroner must be brought, they stubbornly insisted, and they restrained me forcibly when I would have waded into the water. We turned back with shaking knees and hurried toward the mouth of the cave, slipping and sliding in the wet clay as we ran. I, for one, felt as though a dozen assassins were following our footsteps in the dark. And all the time I had a sickening feeling that my uncle's death only foreshadowed a more terrible tragedy. The guide's: "This ain't no accident; it's murder," kept running in my head, and much as I tried to drive the thought from me, a horrible suspicion came creeping to my mind that I knew who the murderer must be.

CHAPTER XI

THE SHERIFF VISITS FOUR-POOLS

We found the coroner and told our story. He sent word to Kennisburg, the county-seat, for the sheriff to come; and then having called a doctor and three or four other witnesses, we set out again for the cave. The news of the tragedy had spread like wild-fire, and half the town of Luray would have accompanied us had the coroner not forcibly prevented it. He stationed two men at the entrance of the cave to keep the crowd from pushing in. I myself should have been more than willing to wait outside, but I felt that it was my duty by Radnor to be present. If any discoveries were made I wished to be the first to know it.

It was sad business and I will not dwell upon it. One side of the old man's head had been fractured by a heavy blow. He had been dead several hours when we found him, but the doctor could not be certain whether drowning, or the injury he had sustained, had been the immediate cause of death. Dangling from a jagged piece of rock half way down the cliff, we found Polly Mathers's coat, torn and drabbled with mud. The clay path above the pool was trampled in every direction 'way out to the brink of the precipice; it was evident, even to the most untrained observer, that a fierce struggle of some sort had taken place. I was the first one to examine the marks, and as I knelt down and held the light to the ground, I saw with a thrill of mingled horror and hope that one pair of feet had been bare. Mose had taken part in the struggle, and dreadful as was the assurance, it was infinitely better than that other suspicion.

"It was Mose who committed the murder!" I cried to the

coroner as I pointed to the foot-prints in the clay.

He bent over beside me and examined the marks.

"Ah——Mose was present," he said slowly, "but so was someone else. See, here is the print of the Colonel's boot and there beside it is the print of another boot; it is fully an inch broader."

But it was difficult to make out anything clearly, so trampled was the path. Our whole party had passed over the very spot not an hour before the tragedy. Whatever the others could see, I, myself, was blind to everything but the indisputable fact that Mose had been there.

As we were making ready to start back to the mouth of the cave, a cry from one of the men called our attention again to the scene of the struggle. He held up in his hand a small, gleaming object which he had found trodden into the path. It was a silver match box covered with dents and mud and marked "R. F. G." I recognized it instantly; I had seen Radnor take it from his pocket a hundred times. As I looked at it now my hope seemed to vanish and that same sickening suspicion rushed over me again. The men eyed each other silently, and I did not have to ask what they were thinking of. We turned without comments and started on our journey back to the village. The body was carried to the hotel to await the coroner's permission to take it home to Four-Pools. There was nothing more for me to do, and with a heavy heart I mounted again to return to the plantation.

Scarcely had I left the stable yard when I heard hoofs pounding along behind me in the darkness, and Jim Mattison galloped up with two of his men.

"If you are going to Four-Pools we will ride with you," he said, falling into pace beside me while the officers dropped behind. "I might as well tell you," he added, "that it looks black for Radnor. I'm sorry, but it's my duty to keep him under arrest until some pretty strong counter-evidence turns up."

"Where's Cat-Eye Mose?" I cried. "Why don't you arrest him?"

The sheriff made a gesture of disdain.

"That's nonsense. Everyone in the county knows Cat-Eye

Mose. He wouldn't hurt a fly. If he was present at the time of the crime it was to help his master, and the man who killed Colonel Gaylord killed him too. I've known him all my life and I can swear he's innocent."

"You've known Radnor all your life," I returned bitterly.

"Yes," he said, "I have—and Jefferson Gaylord, too."

I rode on in silence and I do not think I ever hated anyone as, for the moment, I hated the man beside me. I knew that he was thinking of Polly Mathers, and I imagined that I could detect an undertone of triumph in his voice.

"It's well known," he went on, half to himself and half to me, "that Radnor sometimes had high words with his father; and to-day, they tell me at the hotel, he came back alone without waiting for the others, and while his horse was being saddled he drank off two glasses of brandy as if they had been water. All the men on the veranda marked how white his face was, and how he cursed the stable boy for being slow. It was evident that something had happened in the cave, and what with finding his match box at the scene of the crime—circumstantial evidence is pretty strong against him."

I was too miserable to think of any answer; and, the fellow finally having the decency to keep quiet, we galloped the rest of the way in silence.

Though it must have been long after midnight when we reached the house, lights were still burning in the downstairs rooms. We rode up to the portico with considerable clamor and dismounted. One of the men held the horses while Mattison and the other followed me into the house. Rad himself, hearing the noise of our arrival, came to the door to meet us. He was quite composed again and spoke in his usual manner.

"Hello, Arnold! Did you find him, and is the party over?"

He stopped uncertainly as he caught sight of the others. They stepped into the hall and stood watching him a moment without saying anything. I tried to tell him but the words seemed to stick in my throat.

"A—a terrible thing has happened, Rad," I stammered out.

"What's the matter?" he asked, a sudden look of anxiety springing to his face.

"I am sorry, Rad," Mattison replied, "but it is my duty to arrest you."

"To arrest me, for what?" he asked with a half laugh.

"For the murder of your father."

Radnor put out his hand against the wall to steady himself, and his lips showed white in the lamp light. At the sight of his face I could have sworn that he was not acting, and that the news came with as much of a shock to him as it had to me.

"My father murdered!" he gasped. "What do you mean?"

"His dead body was found in the cave, and circumstantial evidence points to you."

He seemed too dazed to grasp the words and Mattison said it twice before he comprehended.

"Do you mean he's dead?" Rad repeated. "And I quarrelled with him last night and wouldn't make it up—and now it's too late."

"I must warn you," the sheriff returned, "that whatever you say will be used against you."

"I am innocent," said Radnor, brokenly, and without another word he prepared to go. Mattison drew some hand-cuffs from his pocket, and Radnor looked at them with a dark flush.

"You needn't be afraid. I am not going to run away," he said. Mattison dropped them back again with a muttered apology.

I went out to the stable with one of the men and helped to saddle Jennie Loo. I felt all the time as though I had hold of the rope that was going to hang him. When we came back he and the sheriff were standing on the portico, waiting. Rad appeared to be more composed than any of us, but as I wrung his hand I noticed that it was icy cold.

"I'll attend to everything," I said, "and don't worry, my boy. We'll get you off."

"Don't worry!" He laughed shortly as he leaped into the saddle. "It's not myself I'm worrying over; I am innocent," and he suddenly leaned forward and scanned my face in the light from the open door. "You believe me?" he asked quickly.

"Yes," I cried, "I do! And what's more, I'll *prove* you're innocent."

CHAPTER XII

I MAKE A PROMISE TO POLLY

The next few days were a nightmare to me. Even now I cannot think of that horrible period of suspense and doubt without a shudder. The coroner set to work immediately upon his preliminary investigation, and every bit of evidence that turned up only seemed to make the proof stronger against Radnor.

It is strange how ready public opinion is to believe the worst of a man when he is down. No one appeared to doubt Rad's guilt, and feeling ran high against him. Colonel Gaylord was a well-known character in the countryside, and in spite of his quick temper and rather imperious bearing he had been a general favorite. At the news of his death a wave of horror and indignation swept through the valley. Among the roughs in the village I heard not infrequent hints of lynching; and even among the more conservative element, the general opinion seemed to be that lawful hanging was too honorable a death for the perpetrator of so brutal a crime.

I have never been able to understand the quick and general belief in the boy's guilt, but I have always suspected that the sheriff did not do all in his power to quiet the feeling. It was to a large extent, however, the past reasserting itself. Though Radnor's record was not so black as it was painted, still, it was not so white as it should have been. People shook their heads and repeated stories of how wild he had been as a boy, and how they had always foreseen some such end as this. Reports of the quarrels with his father were told and retold until they were magnified beyond all recognition. The old scandals about Jeff were revived again, and the general opinion seemed to be that the Gaylord boys were degenerates through and through. Rad's personal friends stood by him staunchly; but they formed a pitifully small minority compared to the general sensation-seeking public.

I visited Radnor in the Kennisburg jail on the morning of my uncle's funeral and found him quite broken in spirit. He had had time to think over the past, and with his father lying dead at Four-Pools, it had not been pleasant thinking. Now that it was too late, he seemed filled with remorse over his conduct toward the old man, and he dwelt continually on the fact of his having been unwilling to make up the quarrel of the night before the murder. In this mood of contrition he mercilessly accused himself of things I am sure he had never done. I knew that the jailer was listening to every word outside, and I became unspeakably nervous for fear he would say something which could be twisted into an incriminating confession. He did not seem to comprehend in the least the danger of his own position; he was entirely taken up with the horror of his father's death. As I was leaving, however, he suddenly grasped my hand with tears in his eyes.

"Tell me, Arnold, do people really believe me guilty?"

I knew by "people" he meant Polly Mathers; but I had not had an opportunity to speak with her alone since the day of the tragedy.

"I haven't talked to anyone but the sheriff," I returned.

"Mattison would be glad enough to prove it," Radnor said bitterly, and he turned his back and stood staring through the iron bars of the window, while I went out and the jailer closed the door and locked it.

All through the funeral that afternoon I could scarcely keep my eyes from Polly Mathers's face. She appeared so changed since the day of the picnic that I should scarcely have known her for the same person; it seemed incredible that three days could make such a difference in a bright, healthy, vigorous girl. All her youthful vivacity was gone; she was pale and spiritless with deep rings beneath her eyes and the lids red with crying. After the services were over, I approached her a moment as she stood in her black dress aloof from the others at the edge of the little family burying-ground. She greeted me with a tremulous smile, and then as her glance wandered back to the pile of earth that two men were already shoveling into the grave, her eyes quickly filled with tears.

"I loved him as much as if he were my own father," she cried, "and it's my fault that he's dead. I made him go!"

"No, Polly, it is not your fault," I said decisively. "It was a thing which no one could foresee and no one could help."

She waited a moment trying to steady her voice, then she looked up pleadingly in my face.

"Radnor is innocent; tell me you believe it."

"I am sure he is innocent," I replied.

"Then you can clear him—you're a lawyer. I know you can clear him!"

"You may trust me to do my best, Polly."

"I hate Jim Mattison!" she exclaimed, with a flash of her old fire. "He swears that Rad is guilty and that he will prove him so. Rad may have done some bad things, but he's a good man—better than Jim Mattison ever thought of being."

"Polly," I said with a touch of bitterness, "I wish you might have realized that truth earlier. Rad is at heart as splendid a chap as ever lived, and his friends ought never to have allowed him to go astray."

She looked away without answering, and then in a moment turned back to me and held out her hand.

"Good-by. When you see him again please tell him what I said."

As she turned away I looked after her, puzzled. I was sure at last that she was in love with Radnor, and I was equally sure that he did not know it; for in spite of his sorrow at his father's death and of the suspicion that rested on him, I knew that he would not have been so completely crushed had he felt that she was with him. Why must this come to him now too late to do him any good, when he had needed it so much before? I felt momentarily enraged at Polly. It seemed somehow as if the trouble might have been avoided had she been more straightforward. Then at the memory of her pale face and pleading eyes I relented. However thoughtless she had been before, she was changed now; this tragedy had somehow made a woman of her over night. When Radnor came at last to claim her, they would each, perhaps, be worthier of the other.

I returned to the empty house that night and sat down to look the facts squarely in the face. I had hitherto been so occupied with the necessary preparations for the funeral, and with instituting a search for Cat-Eye Mose, that I had scarcely had time to think, let alone map out any logical plan of action. Radnor was so stunned by the blow that he could barely talk coherently, and as yet I had had no satisfactory interview with him.

Immediately after the Colonel's death, I had very hastily run over his private papers, but had found little to suggest a clue. Among some old letters were several from Nannie's husband, written at the time of her sickness and death; their tone was bitter. Could the man have accomplished a tardy revenge for past insults? I asked myself. But investigation showed this theory to be most untenable. He was still living in the little Kansas village where she had died, had married again, and become a peaceful plodding citizen. It required all his present energy to support his wife and children—I dare say the brief episode of his first marriage had almost faded from his mind. There was not the slightest chance that he could be implicated.

I sifted the papers again, thoroughly and painstakingly, but found nothing that would throw any light upon the mystery. While I was still engaged with this task, a message came from the coroner saying that the formal inquest would begin at ten o'clock the next morning in the Kennisburg court-house. This gave me no chance to plan any sort of campaign, and I could do little more than let matters take their course. I hoped however that in the progress of the inquest, some clue would be brought to light which would render Radnor's being remanded for trial impossible.

So far, I had to acknowledge, the evidence against him appeared overwhelming. A motive was supplied in the fact that the Colonel's death would leave him his own master and a rich man. The well-known fact of their frequent quarrels, coupled with Radnor's fierce temper and somewhat revengeful disposition, was a very strong point in his disfavor; added to this, the suspicious circumstances of the day of the tragedy—the fact that he was not with the rest of the party when the crime must have been committed, the alleged print of his boots and the finding of the match box, his subsequent perturbed condition—everything pointed to him as the author of the crime. It was a most convincing chain of circumstantial evidence.

Considering the data that had come to light, there seemed to be only one alternative, and that was that Cat-Eye Mose had committed the murder. I clung tenaciously to this belief; but I found, in the absence of any further proof or any conceivable motive, that few people shared it with me. The marks of his bare feet proved conclusively that he had been, in whatever capacity, an active participator in the struggle.

"He was there to aid his master," the sheriff affirmed, "and being a witness to the crime, it was necessary to put him out of the way."

"Why hide the body of one and not the other?" I asked.

"To throw suspicion on Mose."

This was the universal opinion; no one, from the beginning, would listen to a word against Mose. In his case, as well as in Radnor's, the past was speaking. Through all his life, they said, he had faithfully loved and served the Colonel, and if necessity required, he would willingly have died for him.

But for myself, I continued to believe in the face of all opposition, that Mose was guilty. It was more a matter of feeling with me than of reasoning. I had always been suspicious of the fellow; a man with eyes like that was capable of anything. The objection which the sheriff raised that Colonel Gaylord was both larger and stronger than Mose and could easily have overcome him, proved nothing to my mind. Mose was a small man, but he was long-armed and wirey, doubtless far stronger than he looked; besides, he had been armed, and the nature of his weapon was clear. The floor of the cave was strewn with scores of broken stalactites; nothing could have made a more formidable weapon than one of these long pieces of jagged stone used as a club.

As to the motive for the crime, who could tell what went on in the slow workings of his mind? The Colonel had struck him more than once—unjustly, I did not doubt—and though he seemed at the moment to take it meekly, might he not have been merely biding his time? His final revenge may have been the outcome of many hoarded grievances that no one knew existed. The fellow was more than half insane. What more likely than that he had attacked his master in a fit of animal passion; and then, terrified at the result, escaped to the woods? That seemed to me the only plausible explanation.

No facts had come out concerning the ha'nt or the robbery, and I do not think that either was connected in the public mind with the murder. But to my mind the death of Colonel Gaylord was but the climax of the long series of events which commenced on the night of my arrival with the slight and ludicrous episode of the stolen roast chicken. I had been convinced at the time that Mose was at the bottom of it, and I was convinced now that he was also at the bottom of the robbery and the murder. How Radnor had got drawn into the muddle of the ha'nt, I could not fathom; but I suspected that Mose had hoodwinked him as he had the rest of us.

Assuming that my theory was right, then Mose was hiding; and all my energies from the beginning had been bent toward his discovery. The low range of mountains which lay between Four-Pools Plantation and the Luray valley was covered thickly with woods and very sparsely settled. Mose knew every foot of the ground; he had wandered over these mountains for days at a time, and must have been familiar with many hiding places. It was in this region that I hoped to find him.

Immediately after the Colonel's death I had offered a large reward either for Mose's capture, or for any information regarding his whereabouts. His description had been telegraphed all up and down the valley and every farmer was on the alert. Bands of men had been formed and the woods scoured for him, but as yet without result. I was hourly expecting, however, that some clue would come to light.

The sheriff, on the other hand, in pursuance of his theory that Mose had been murdered, had been no less indefatigable in his search for the body. The river had been dragged, the cave and surrounding woods searched, but nothing had been found. Mose had simply vanished from the earth and left no trace.

To my disappointment the morning still brought no news; I had hoped to have something definite before the inquest opened. I rode into Kennisburg early in order to hold a conference with Radnor, and get from him the facts in regard to his own and Mose's connection with the ha'nt. My former passivity in the matter struck me now as almost criminal; perhaps had I insisted in probing it to the bottom, my uncle might have been living still. I entered Radnor's cell determined not to leave it until I knew the truth.

But I met with an unexpected obstacle. He refused absolutely to discuss the question.

"Radnor," I cried at last, "are you trying to shield any one? Do you know who killed your father?"

"I know no more about who killed my father than you do."

"Do you know about the ha'nt?"

"Yes," he said desperately, "I do; but it is not connected with either the robbery or the murder and I cannot talk about it."

I argued and pleaded but to no effect. He sat on his cot, his head in his hands staring at the floor, stubbornly refusing to open his lips. I gave over pleading and stormed.

"It's no use, Arnold," he said finally. "I won't tell you anything about the ha'nt; it doesn't enter into the case."

I sat down again and patiently outlined my theory in regard to Mose.

"It is impossible," he declared. "I have known Mose all my life, and I have never yet known him to betray a trust. He loved my father as much as I did, and if my life depended on it, I should swear that he was faithful."

"Rad," I beseeched, "I am not only your attorney, I am your friend; whatever you say to me is as if it had never been said. I *must* know the truth."

He shook his head.

"I have nothing to say."

"You have *got* to have something to say," I cried. "You have got to go on the stand and make an absolutely open and straightforward statement of everything bearing on the case. You have got to appear anxious to find and punish the man who murdered your father. You have got to gain public sympathy, and before you go on the stand you owe it to yourself and me to leave nothing unexplained between us."

He raised his eyes miserably to mine.

"Must I go on?" he asked. "Can't I refuse to testify—I don't see that they can punish me for contempt of court; I'm already in prison."

"They can hang you," said I, bluntly.

He buried his face in his hands with a groan.

"Arnold," he pleaded, "don't make me face all those people. You can see what a state my nerves are in; I haven't slept for three nights." He held out his hand to show me how it trembled. "I can't talk—I don't know what I'm saying. You don't know what you're urging me to do."

My anger at his stubbornness vanished in a sudden spasm of pity. The poor fellow was scarcely more than a boy! Though I was completely in the dark as to what he was holding back and why he was doing it, yet I felt instinctively that his motives were honorable.

"Rad," I said, "it would help your cause to be open with me, and if you are remanded for trial before the grand jury you must in the end tell me everything. But now I will not insist. Probably nothing will come up about the ha'nt. I can of course refuse to let you speak on the ground of incriminating evidence, but that is the last stand I wish to take. We must gain public opinion on our side and to that end you must testify yourself. You must force every person present to believe that you are incapable of telling a falsehood—I believe that already and so does Polly Mathers."

Radnor's face flushed and a quick light sprang into his eyes.

"What do you mean?"

I repeated what Polly had said and I added my own interpretation. The effect was electrical. He straightened his shoulders with an air of trying to throw off his despondency.

"I'll do my best," he promised. "Heaven knows I'd like to know the truth as well as you—this doubt is simply hell!"

A knock sounded on the door and a sheriff's officer informed us that the hearing was about to begin.

"You haven't explained your actions on the day of the murder," I said hurriedly. "I must have a reason."

"That's all right—it will come out. If you just keep 'em off the ha'nt, I'll clear everything else."

"If you do that," said I, immeasurably relieved, "there'll be no danger of your being held for trial." I rose and held out my hand. "Courage, my boy; remember that you are going to prove your innocence, not only for your own, but for Polly's sake."

CHAPTER XIII

THE INQUEST

The coroner's court was packed; and though here and there I caught a face that I knew to be friendly to Radnor, the crowd was made up for the most part of morbid sensation seekers, eager to hear and believe the worst.

The District Attorney was present; indeed he and the coroner and Jim Mattison were holding a whispered consultation when I entered the room, and I did not doubt but that the three had been working up the case together. The thought was not reassuring; a coroner, with every appearance of fairness, may still bias a jury by the form his questions take. And I myself was scarcely in a position to turn the trend of the inquiry; I doubt if a lawyer ever went to an inquisition with less command of the facts than I had.

The first witness called was the doctor who made the autopsy. After his testimony had been dwelt upon with what seemed to me needless detail, the facts relating to the finding of the body were brought forward. From this, the investigation veered to the subject of Radnor's strange behavior on the afternoon of the murder. The landlord, stable boy and several hangers-on of the Luray Hotel were called to the stand; their testimony was practically identical, and I did not attempt to question its truth.

"What time did Radnor Gaylord come back to the hotel?" the coroner asked of "old man Tompkins," the landlord.

"I reckon it must 'a' been 'long about three in the afternoon."

"Please describe exactly what occurred."

"Well, we was sittin' on the veranda talkin' about one thing and another when we see young Gaylord comin' across the lot, his head down and his hands in his pockets walkin' fast. He yelled to Jake, who was washin' off a buggy at the pump, to saddle his horse and be quick about it. Then he come up the steps and into the bar-room and called for brandy. He drunk two glasses straight off without blinkin'."

"Had he ordered anything to drink in the morning when they left their horses?" the coroner interrupted at this point.

"No, he didn't go into the bar-room—and it wasn't usually his custom to slight us either."

A titter ran around the room and the coroner rapped for order. "This is not the place for any cheap witticisms; you will kindly confine yourself to answering my questions.—Did Mr. Gaylord appear to have been drinking when he returned from the cave?"

The landlord closed his right eye speculatively. "No, I can't say as he exactly appeared like he'd been drinking," he said with the air of a connoisseur, "but he did seem to be considerably upset about something. He looked mad enough to bite; his face was pale, and his hand trembled when he raised his glass. Three or four noticed it and wondered—"

"Very well," interrupted the coroner, "what did he do next?"

"He went out to the stable yard and swore at the boy for being slow. And he tightened the surcingle himself with such a jerk that the mare plunged and he struck her. He is usually pretty cranky about the way horses is treated, and we wondered—"

He was stopped again and invited to go on without wondering.

"Well, let me see," said the witness, imperturbably. "He jumped into the saddle and slashing the mare across the flanks, started off in a cloud o' dust, without so much as looking back. We was all surprised at this 'cause he's usually pretty friendly, and we talked about it after; but we didn't think nothing particular till the news o' the murder come that evening, when we naturally commenced to put two and two together."

At this point I protested and the landlord was excused. "Jake" Henley, the stable boy, was called. His testimony practically covered the same ground and corroborated what the landlord had said.

"You say he swore at you for being slow?" the coroner asked.

Jake nodded with a grin. "I don't remember just the words—I get swore at so much that it don't make the impression it might—but it was good straight cussin' all right."

"And he struck you as being agitated?"

Jake's grin broadened. "I think you might say agitated," he admitted guardedly. "He was mad enough to begin with, an' now the brandy was gettin' to work. Besides, he was in an all-fired hurry to leave before the rest o' the party come back, an' while I was bringin' out the horse, he heard 'em laughin'. They wasn't in sight yet, but they was makin' a lot o' noise. One o' the girls had stepped on a snake an' was squealin' loud enough to hear her two miles off."

"And Gaylord left before any of them saw him?"

The boy nodded. "He got off all right. 'You forgot to pay for your horse,' I yelled after him, and he threw me fifty cents and it landed in the watering-trough."

This ended his testimony.

Several members of the picnic party were next called upon, and nothing very damaging to Radnor was produced. He seemed to be in his usual spirits before entering the cave, and no one, it transpired, had seen him after he came out, though this was not noted at the time. Also, no one had noticed him in conversation with his father. The coroner dwelt upon this point, but elicited no information one way or the other.

Polly Mathers was not present. She had been subpœnaed, but had become too ill and nervous to stand the strain, and the doctor had forbidden her attendance. The coroner, however, had taken her testimony at the house, and his clerk read it aloud to the jury. It dealt merely with the matter of the coat and where she had last seen Radnor.

"*Question.* 'Did you notice anything peculiar in the behavior of Radnor Gaylord on the day of his father's death?'

"*Answer.* 'Nothing especially peculiar—no.'

"Q. 'Did you see any circumstance which led you to suspect that he and his father were not on good terms?'

"A. 'No, they both appeared as usual.'

"Q. 'Did you speak to Radnor in the cave?'

"A. 'Yes, we strolled about together for a time and he was carrying my coat. He laid it down on the broken column and forgot it. I forgot it too and didn't think of it again until we were out of the cave. Then I happened to mention it in Colonel Gaylord's presence, and I suppose he went back for it.'

"Q. 'You didn't see Radnor Gaylord after he left the cave?'

"A. 'No, I didn't see him after we left the gallery of the broken column. The guide struck off a calcium light to show us the formation of the ceiling. We spent about five minutes examining the room, and after that we all went on in a group. Radnor had not waited to see the room, but had gone on ahead in the direction of the entrance.'"

So much for Polly's testimony—which added nothing.

Solomon, frightened almost out of his wits, was called on next, and his testimony brought out the matter of the quarrel between Colonel Gaylord and Radnor. Solomon told of finding the French clock, and a great many things besides which I am sure he made up. I wished to have his testimony ruled out, but the coroner seemed to feel that it was suggestive—as it undoubtedly was—and he allowed it to remain.

Radnor himself was next called to the stand. As he took his place a murmur of excitement swept over the room and there was a general straining forward. He was composed and quiet, and very very sober—every bit of animation had left his face.

The coroner commenced immediately with the subject of the quarrel with his father on the night before the murder, and Radnor answered all the questions frankly and openly. He made no attempt to gloss over any of the details. What put the matter in a peculiarly bad light, was the fact that the cause of the quarrel had been over a question of money. Rad had requested his father to settle a definite amount on him so that he would be independent in the future, and his father had refused. They had lost their tempers and had gone further than usual; in telling the story Radnor openly took the blame upon himself where, in several instances, I strongly suspected that it should have been laid at the door of the Colonel. But in spite of the fact that the story revealed a pitiable state of affairs as between father and son, his frankness in assuming the responsibility won for him more sympathy than had been shown since the murder.

"How did the clock get broken?" the coroner asked.

"My father knocked it off the mantelpiece onto the floor."

"He did not throw it at you as Solomon surmised?"

Radnor raised his head with a glint of anger.

"It fell on the floor and broke."

"Have you often had quarrels with your father?"

"Occasionally. He had a quick temper and always wished his own way, and I was not so patient with him as I should have been."

"What did you quarrel about?"

"Different things."

"What, for instance?"

"Sometimes because he thought I spent too much money, sometimes over a question of managing the estate; occasionally because he had heard gossip about me."

"What do you mean by 'gossip'?"

"Stories that I'd been gambling or drinking too much."

"Were the stories true?"

"They were always exaggerated."

"And this quarrel the night before his death was more serious than usual?"

"Possibly—yes."

"You did not speak to each other at the breakfast table?"

"No."

Radnor's face was set in strained lines; it was evident that this was a very painful subject.

"Did you have any conversation later?"

"Only a few words."

"Please repeat what was said."

Radnor appeared to hesitate and then replied a trifle wearily that he did not remember the exact words; that it was merely a recapitulation of what had been said the night before. Upon being urged to give the gist of the conversation he replied that his father had wished to make up their quarrel, but on the old basis, and he had refused. The Colonel had repeated that he was still too young a man to give over his affairs into the hands of another,—that he had a good many years before him in which he intended to be his own master. Radnor had replied that he was too old a man to be treated any longer as a boy, and that he would go away and work where he would be paid for what he did.

"And may I ask," the coroner inquired placidly, "whether you had any particular work in mind when you made that statement, or was it merely a figure of rhetoric calculated to bring Colonel Gaylord to terms?"

Rad scowled and said nothing, and the rest of his answers were terseness itself.

"Did you and your father have any further conversation on the ride over, or in the course of the day?"

"No."

"You purposely avoided meeting each other?"

"I suppose so."

"Then those words after breakfast when you threatened to leave home were absolutely the last words you ever spoke to your father?"

It was a subject Radnor did not like to think about. His lips trembled slightly and he answered with a visible effort.

"Yes."

A slight murmur ran around the room, partly of sympathy, partly of doubt.

The coroner put the same question again and Radnor repeated his answer, this time with a flush of anger. The coroner paused a moment and then continued without comment:

"You entered the cave with the rest of the party?"

"Yes."

"But you left the others before they had made the complete round?"

"Yes."

"Why was that?"

"I was not particularly interested. I had seen the cave many times before."

"Where did you leave the party?"

"I believe in the gallery of the broken column."

"You left the cave immediately?"

"Yes."

"Did you enter it again?"

"No."

"You forgot Miss Mathers's coat and left it in the gallery of the broken column?"

"So it would seem."

"Did you not think of that later and go back for it?"

Radnor snapped out his answer. "No, I didn't think anything about the coat."

"Are you in the habit of leaving young ladies' coats about in that off-hand way?"

A titter ran about the room, and Rad did not deign to notice this question.

I was indignant that the boy should be made to face such an ordeal. This was not a regular trial and the coroner had no right to be more obnoxious than his calling required. There was a glint of anger in Radnor's eyes; and I was uneasily aware that he no longer cared what impression he made. His answers to the rest of the questions were as short as the English language permitted.

"What did you do after leaving the cave?"

"Went home."

"Please go into more detail. What did you do immediately after leaving the cave?"

"Strolled through the woods."

"For how long?"

"I don't know."

"How long do you think?"

"Possibly half an hour."

"Then what did you do?"

"Returned to the hotel, ordered my horse and rode home."

"Why did you not wait for the rest of the party?"

"Didn't feel like it."

The question was repeated in several ways, but Radnor stubbornly refused to discuss the matter. He had promised me, the last thing before coming to the hearing, that he would clear up the suspicious points in regard to his conduct on the day of the crime. I took him in hand myself, but I could get nothing more from him than the coroner had elicited. For some reason he had veered completely, and his manner warned me not to push the matter. I took my seat and the questioning continued.

"Mr. Gaylord," said the coroner, severely, "you have heard the evidence respecting your peculiar behavior when you returned to the hotel. Three witnesses have stated that you were in an unnaturally perturbed condition. Is this true?"

Radnor supposed it must be true. He did not wish to question the gentlemen's veracity. He did not remember himself what he had done, but there seemed to be plenty of witnesses who did remember.

"Can you give any reasons for your strange conduct?"

"I have told you several times already that I can not. I did not feel well, and that is all there was to it."

A low murmur of incredulity ran around the room. It was evident to everyone that he was holding something back, and I could see that he was fast losing the sympathy he had gained in the beginning. I myself was at a loss to account for his behavior; as I was absolutely in the dark, however, I could do nothing but let matters take their course. Radnor was excused with this, and the next half hour was spent in a consideration of the foot-prints that were found in the clay path at the scene of the murder. The marks of Cat-Eye Mose were admitted immediately, but the others occasioned considerable discussion. Facsimiles of the prints were produced and compared with the riding boots which the Colonel and Radnor had worn at the time. The Colonel's print was unmistakable, but I myself did not think that the alleged print of Radnor's boot tallied very perfectly with the boot itself. The jury seemed satisfied however, and Radnor was called upon for an explanation. His only conjecture was that it was the print he had left when he passed over the path on his way to the entrance.

The print was not in the path, he was informed; it was in the wet clay on the edge of the precipice.

Radnor shrugged. In that case it could not be the print of his boot. He had kept to the path.

In regard to the match box he was equally unsatisfactory. He acknowledged that it was his, but could no more account for its presence in the path than the coroner himself.

"When do you remember having seen it last?" the coroner inquired.

Radnor pondered. "I remember lending it to Mrs. Mathers when she was building a fire in the woods to make the coffee; after that I don't remember anything about it."

"How do you account for its presence at the scene of the murder?"

"I can only conjecture that it must have dropped from my pocket without my noticing it on my way out of the cave."

The coroner observed that it was an unfortunate coincidence that he had dropped it in just that particular spot.

This effectually stopped Radnor's testimony. Not another word could be elicited from him on the subject, and he was finally dismissed and Mrs. Mathers called to the stand.

She remembered borrowing the match box, but then someone had called her away and she could not remember what she had done with it. She thought she must have returned it because she always did return things, but she was not at all sure. Very possibly she had kept it, and dropped it herself on her way out of the cave.

It was evident that she did not wish to say anything which would incriminate Radnor; and she was really too perturbed to remember what she had done. Several other people were questioned, but no further light could be thrown on the subject of the match box; and so it remained in the end, as it had been in the beginning, merely a very nasty piece of circumstantial evidence.

This ended the hearing for the day, and the inquest was postponed until ten o'clock the following morning. So far, no word had been dropped touching the ha'nt, but I was filled with apprehension as to what the next day would bring forth. I knew that if the subject came up, it would end once for all Radnor's chances of escaping trial before the grand jury. And that would mean, at the best, two months more of prison. What it would mean at the worst I did not like to consider.

CHAPTER XIV

THE JURY'S VERDICT

My first glance about the room the next morning, showed me only too plainly what direction the inquiry was going to take. In the farther corner half hidden by Mattison's broad back sat Clancy, the Washington detective. I recognized him with an angry feeling of discouragement. If we were to have his version of the stolen bonds, Radnor's last hope of gaining public sympathy was gone.

Radnor was the first person to be called to the stand. He had not noticed the detective, and I did not have a chance to inform him of his presence. The coroner plunged immediately into the question of the robbery and the ha'nt, and it was only too evident from Radnor's troubled eyes that it was a subject he did not wish to talk about.

"You have recently had a robbery at your house, Mr. Gaylord?"

"Yes."

"Please describe just what was stolen."

"Five bonds—Government four per cents—a bag of coin—about twenty dollars in all—and two deeds and an insurance policy."

"You have not been able to trace the thief?"

"No."

"In spite of every effort?"

"Well, we naturally looked into the matter."

"But you have been able to form no theory as to how the bonds were stolen?"

"No, I have no theory whatever."

"You employed a detective I believe?"

"Yes."

"And he arrived at no theory?"

Radnor hesitated visibly while he framed an answer.

"He arrived at no theory which successfully covered the facts."

"But he did have a theory as to the whereabouts of the bonds, did he not?"

"Yes—but it was without any foundation and I prefer not to go into it."

The coroner abandoned the point. "Mr. Gaylord, there has lately been a rumor among the negroes working at your place, in regard to the appearance of a ghost, has there not?"

"Yes."

"Can you offer any light on the subject?"

"The negroes are superstitious and easily frightened, when the rumor of a ghost gets started it grows. The most of the stories existed only in their own imaginations."

"You believe then that there was no foundation whatever to any of the stories?"

"I should rather not go into that."

"Mr. Gaylord, do you believe that the ghost had any connection with the robbery?"

"No, I do not."

"Do you think that the ghost had any connection with the murder of your father?"

"No!" said Radnor.

"That is all, Mr. Gaylord.—James Clancy."

At the name Radnor suddenly raised his head and half turned back as if to speak, but thinking better of it, he resumed his chair and watched the approach of the detective with an angry frown. Clancy did not glance at Radnor, but gave his evidence in a quick incisive way which forced the breathless attention of every one in the room. He told without interruption the story of his arrival at Four-Pools and his conclusions in regard to the ha'nt and the theft; he omitted, however, all mention of the letter.

"Am I to understand that you never made your conclusions known to Colonel Gaylord?" the coroner asked.

"No, I had been employed by him, but I thought under the circumstances it was kinder to leave him in ignorance."

"That was a generous stand to take. I suppose you lost something in the way of a fee?"

The detective looked slightly uncomfortable over the question.

"Well, no, as it happened I didn't. There was a sort of cousin—Mr. Crosby"—he nodded toward me—"visiting in the house and he footed the bill. He seemed to think the young man hadn't intended to steal, and that it would be pleasanter all around if I left it for them to settle between themselves."

"I protest!" I cried. "I distinctly stated my conviction that Radnor Gaylord knew nothing of the bonds, and I paid him to get rid of him because I did not wish him troubling Colonel Gaylord with any such made-up story."

"Mr. Clancy is testifying," observed the coroner. "Now, Mr. Clancy, as I understand it, you discovered as you supposed the guilty man, and instead of going to your employer with the story and receiving your pay from him, you accepted it from the person you had accused—or at least from his friend?"

"I've explained the circumstances; it was a mere matter of accommodation."

"I suppose you know what such accommodation is called?"

"If you mean it was blackmail—that's false! At least," he added, quickly relapsing into good nature, "it was a mighty generous kind of blackmail. I could have got my pay fast enough from the Colonel but I didn't want to stir up trouble. We all know that it isn't the innocent who pay blackmail," he added parenthetically.

"Do you mean to insinuate that Mr. Crosby is implicated?"

"Lord no! He's as innocent as a lamb. Young Gaylord was too smart for him; he hoodwinked him as well as the Colonel into believing the bonds were stolen while he was out of the house."

A smile ran around the room and the detective was excused. I sprang to my feet.

"One moment!" I said. "I should like to ask Mr. Clancy some questions."

The young man was turned over to me, plainly against his wishes.

"What proof have you, Mr. Clancy, that the bonds were not stolen while Mr. Gaylord was out of the house?"

"Well, my investigations led me to the belief that he stole them, and that being the case, it must have been done before he left the house."

"I see! And your investigations concerned themselves largely with a letter which you filched from Mr. Gaylord's coat pocket in the night, did they not?"

"Not entirely—the letter merely struck me as corroborative evidence, though I have since learned—"

"Mr. Clancy," I interrupted sternly, "did you not tell me at the time, that that letter was absolute proof of his guilt—yes or no?"

"I may have said so but—"

"Mr. Clancy, will you kindly repeat what was in that letter."

"It referred to some bonds; I don't know that I can recall the exact words."

"Then I must request you to read it," I returned, picking it out from a bundle of papers on the table and handing it to him. "I am sorry to take up so much time with a matter that has nothing to do with the murder," I added to the coroner, "but you yourself brought up the subject and it is only fair to hear the whole story."

He nodded permission, and ordered Clancy to read the letter. The detective did so amidst an astonished hush. It struck everyone as a proof of guilt, and no one could understand why I had forced it to the front.

"Now Mr. Clancy," said I, "please tell the jury Mr. Gaylord's explanation of this letter."

Clancy with a somewhat sheepish air gave the gist of what Radnor had said.

"Did you believe that story when you first heard it?" I asked.

"No," said he, "I did not, because—"

"Very well! But you later went to the office of Jacoby, Haight & Co., and looked over the files of their correspondence with Radnor Gaylord and verified his statement in every particular, did you not?"

"Yes, I did, but still—"

"That is all I wish to ask, Mr. Clancy. I think the reason is evident," I added, turning to the jury, "why I was willing to pay in order to get rid of him. Nobody's character, nobody's correspondence, was safe while he was in the house."

The detective retired amidst general laughter and I could see that feeling had veered again in Radnor's favor. The total effect of the evidence respecting the ha'nt and the robbery was good rather than bad, and I more than fancied that I was indebted to the sheriff for it.

Radnor was not called again and that was the end of the testimony in regard to him. The rest of the time was taken up with a consideration of Cat-Eye Mose and some further questioning of the negroes in regard to the ha'nt. Old Nancy created considerable diversion with her account of the spirited roast chicken. It had changed materially since I heard it last. She was emphatic in her statement that "Marse Rad didn't have nuffen to do wif him. He was a sho' nuff ha'nt an' his gahments smelt o' de graveyard."

The evidence respecting Mose brought out nothing of any consequence, and with that the hearing was brought to a close. The coroner instructed the jury on two or three points of law and ended with the brief formula:

"You have heard the testimony given by these witnesses. It remains for you to do your duty."

After an interminable half hour the jury-men filed back to their seats and the clerk read the verdict:

"We find that the said Richard Gaylord came to his death in Luray Cavern on the 19th day of May, by cerebral hemorrhage, the result of a wound inflicted by some blunt weapon in the hands of a person or persons unknown. We recommend that

Radnor Fanshaw Gaylord be held for trial before the Grand Jury."

Rad appeared dazed at the verdict; though in the face of the evidence and his own stubborn refusal to explain it, I don't see how he could have expected any other outcome. As for myself, it was better than I had feared.

CHAPTER XV

FALSE CLUES

The fight had now fairly begun. The district attorney was working up the side of the prosecution, aided, I was sure, by the over-zealous sheriff. It remained for me to map out some definite plan of action and organize the defence.

As I rode back to Four-Pools in the early evening after the inquest, I continued to dwell upon the evidence, searching blindly for some clue. The question which returned most persistently to my mind was "What has become of Cat-Eye Mose?" It was clear now that upon the answer to this question hinged the ultimate solution of the mystery. I still clung to the belief that he was guilty and in hiding. But five days had elapsed since the murder, and no trace of him had been discovered. It seemed incredible that a man, however well he might know his ground, could, with a whole county on his track, elude detection so effectually.

Supposing after all that he were not guilty, but the sheriff's theory that he had been killed and the body concealed, were true; then who, besides Radnor, could have had any motive for committing the crime? There was nothing from the past that afforded even the suggestion of a clue. The old man seemed to have had no enemies but his sons. His sons? The thought of Jeff suddenly sprang into my mind. If anyone on earth owed the Colonel a grudge it was his elder son. And Jeff had more than his share of the Gaylord spirit which could not lightly forgive an injury. Could he have returned secretly to the neighborhood, and, following his father into the cave, have quarreled with him? Heaven knows he had cause enough! He may, in his anger, have struck the old man without knowing what he was doing, and overcome with horror at the result, have left him and fled.

I was almost as reluctant to believe him guilty of the crime as to believe it of Radnor, but the thought having once come, would not be dismissed. I knew that he had sunk pretty low in the nine years since his disappearance, but I could never think of him otherwise than as I myself remembered him. He had been the hero of my boyhood and I revolted from the thought of deliberately setting out to prove him guilty of his father's murder.

I spurred my horse into a gallop, miserably trying to escape from my suspicion; but the more I put it from me as impossible, the surer I became that at last I had stumbled on a clue. Automatically, I began adjusting the evidence to fit this new theory, and reluctant as I was to see it, every circumstance from the beginning fitted it perfectly.

Jeff had returned secretly to the neighborhood, had taken up his abode in the old negro cabins and made his presence known only to Mose. Mose had stolen the chicken for him, and the various other missing articles. They had resurrected the ha'nt to frighten the negroes away from the laurel walk, and the night of the party Rad, in his masquerade, had accidentally discovered his brother. Jeff demanded money, and Rad undertook to supply it in order to get him away without his father's knowing. That was why he had borrowed the hundred dollars from me, and had written to his brokers to sell the bonds. It was Jeff who was sitting beside Radnor the night they drove across the lawn. But unknown to Rad, Jeff had found his way back and had robbed the safe, and Rad suspecting it, had refused to make an investigation.

During the eleven days that intervened between the robbery and the murder Jeff had still been hiding in the vicinity—possibly in the neighborhood of Luray, certainly no longer in the cabins, for he had no desire to meet his brother.

But on the day of the picnic they had met and quarreled. Rad had charged him with the robbery and they had parted in a high state of anger. This would explain Rad's actions in the hotel, his white face later when I found him in the summer house. And Jeff, still quivering from the boy's accusation, had gone back into the cave and met his father as the old man was coming from the little gallery of the broken column with Polly Mathers's coat. What had happened there I did not like to consider; they both had uncontrolled tempers, and in the past there had been wrongs on both sides. Probably Jeff's blow had been harder than he meant.

In the evening when Mattison and I brought the news of the murder, Rad must have known instantly who was the real culprit. That was why he had kept silent; that was why he so vehemently insisted on Mose's innocence. I had found the light at last—though the darkness had been almost better.

What must I do? I asked myself. Was it my duty to search out Jefferson and convict him of this crime? No one could tell what provocation he may have had. Why not let matters take their course? There was nothing but circumstantial evidence against Radnor. Surely no jury would convict him on that. I could work up a sufficient case against Mose to assure his acquittal. He would be released with a blot on his name, he would be regarded for the rest of his life with suspicion; but in any event there seemed to be no outcome which would not involve the family in endless trouble and disgrace. And besides, if he himself elected to be silent, had I any right to speak? Then I pulled myself together. Yes, it was not only right for me to speak; it was my duty. Rad should not be allowed to sacrifice himself. The truth, at whatever cost, must be brought out.

My first move must be to discover Jeff's whereabouts on the day of his father's murder. It ought not to be difficult to trace a man who had come more than once under the surveillance of the police. Having made up my mind as to the necessary course, I lost no time in putting it into action. I barely waited to snatch a hasty supper before riding back to the village. From there I sent a fifty-word telegram to the chief of police in Seattle asking for any information as to the whereabouts of Jefferson Gaylord on the nineteenth of May.

It was ten o'clock the next morning before an answer came. So sure was I of what it was going to contain, that I read the words twice before comprehending them.

> "Jefferson Gaylord spent May nineteenth in lumber camp thirty miles from Seattle. Well-known character. Mistaken identity impossible.
>
> "Henry Waterson,
> "*Police Commissioner.*"

I had become so obsessed with the horror of my new theory; so sure that Jeff was the murderer of his father that I could not readjust my thoughts to the idea that he had been at the time of the crime three thousand miles away. The case, then, still stood exactly where it had stood from the beginning. Six days had passed since the murder and I was not one inch nearer the truth. Six days! I realized it with a dull feeling of hopelessness. Every day now that was allowed to pass only lessened the chance of our ever finding Mose and solving the mystery.

I still stood with the telegram in my hand staring at the words. I was vaguely aware that a boy from "Miller's place" had ridden up to the house on a bicycle, but not until Solomon approached with a second yellow envelope in his hand was I jostled back into a state of comprehension.

"Nurr telegram, Mars' Arnold."

I snatched it from him and ripped it open, hoping against hope that at last a clue had turned up.

> "New York, May 25.
>
> "Post-Dispatch wants correspondent on spot. If you have any facts to give out, save them for me. Arrive Lambert Junction three-fifty.

"Terence K. Patten."

Under the terrible strain of the past six days I had completely forgotten Terry's existence and now the memory of his cool impertinence came back to me with a rush. For the first moment I felt too angry to think; I had not credited even his presumption with anything like this. His interference in the Patterson-Pratt business was bad enough, but he might have realized that this was a personal matter. He was calmly proposing to turn this horrible tragedy into a story for the Sunday papers—and that to a member of the murdered man's own family. Hot with indignation, I tore the telegram into shreds and stalked into the house. I paced up and down the hall for fifteen minutes, planning what I should say to him when he arrived; and then, as I calmed down, I commenced to see the thing in its true light.

The whole account of the crime to the minutest detail, had already appeared in every newspaper in the country, together with the most outrageous stories of Radnor's past career. At least nothing could be worse than what had already been said. And after all, was not the truth—any truth—better than these vague suspicions, this terrible suspense? Terry could find the truth if any man on earth could do it. He had, I knew, unraveled other tangles as mysterious as this. He was used to this sort of work, and bringing to the matter a fresh mind, would see light where it was only darkness to me. I had been under such a terrific strain for so long and had borne so much responsibility, that the very thought of having someone with whom I could share it gave me new strength. My feeling toward him veered suddenly from indignation to gratitude. His irrepressible confidence in himself inspired me with a like confidence, and I wondered what I had been thinking of that I had not sent for him at once. To my jaded mind his promised arrival appeared better than a clue—it was almost equal to a solution.

CHAPTER XVI

TERRY COMES

The moment I caught sight of Terry as he swung off the train I felt involuntarily that my troubles were near their end. His sharp, eager face with its firm jaw and quick eye inspired one with the feeling that he could find the bottom of any mystery. It was with a deep breath of relief that I held out my hand.

"Hello, old man! How are you?" he exclaimed with a smile of cordiality as he grasped it. And then recalling the gravity of the situation, he with some difficulty pulled a sober face. "I'm sorry that we meet again under such sad circumstances," he added perfunctorily. "I suppose you think I've meddled enough in your affairs already; and on my word, I intended to stay out of this. But of course I've been watching it in the papers; partly because it was interesting and partly because I knew you. It struck me yesterday afternoon as I was thinking things over that you weren't making much headway and might like a little help; so I induced the Post-Dispatch to send down their best man. I hope I shall get at the truth." He paused a moment and looked at me sharply. "Do you want me to stay? I will go back if you'd rather have me."

I was instantly ashamed of my distrust of the afternoon. Whatever might be Terry's failings, I could not doubt, as I looked into his face, that his Irish heart was in the right place.

"I am not afraid of the truth," I returned steadily. "If you can discover it, for Heaven's sake do so!"

"That's what I'm paid for," said Terry. "The Post-Dispatch doesn't deal in fiction any more than it can help."

As we climbed into the carriage he added briskly, "It's a

horrible affair! The details as I have them from the papers are not full enough, but you can tell them to me as we drive along."

I should have laughed had I been feeling less anxious. His greeting was so entirely characteristic in the way he shuffled through the necessary condolences and jumped, with such evident relish, to the gruesome details.

As I gathered up the reins and backed away from the hitching-post, Terry broke out with:

"Here, hold on a minute. Where are you going?"

"Back to Four-Pools," I said in some surprise. "I thought you'd want to unpack your things and get settled."

"Haven't much time to get settled," he laughed. "I have an engagement in New York the day after to-morrow. How about the cave? Is it too late to visit it now?"

"Well," I said dubiously, "it's ten miles across the mountains and pretty heavy roads. It would be dark before we got there."

"As far as that goes, we could visit the cave at night as well as in the daytime. But I want to examine the neighborhood and interview some of the people; so I suppose," he added with an impatient sigh, "we'll have to wait till morning. And now, where's this young Gaylord?"

"He's in the Kennisburg jail."

"And where's that?"

"About three miles from here and six miles from the plantation."

"Ah—suppose we pay him a visit first. There are one or two points concerning his whereabouts on the night of the robbery and his actions on the day of the murder that I should like to have him clear up."

I smiled slightly as I turned the horses' heads toward Kennisburg. Radnor in his present uncommunicative frame of mind was not likely to afford Terry much satisfaction.

"There isn't any time to waste," he added as we drove along. "Just let me have your account of everything that happened, beginning with the first appearance of the ghost."

I briefly sketched the situation at Four-Pools as I had found it on my arrival, and the events preceding the robbery and the murder. Terry interrupted me once or twice with questions. He was particularly interested in the three-cornered situation concerning Radnor, Polly Mathers, and Jim Mattison, and I was as brief as possible in my replies; I did not care to make Polly the heroine of a Sunday feature article. He was also persistent in regard to Jefferson's past. I told him all I knew, added the story of my own suspicions, and ended by producing the telegram proving his alibi.

"H'm!" said Terry folding it thoughtfully and putting it in his pocket. "It had occurred to me too that Jeff might be our man—this puts an end to the theory that he personally committed the murder. There are some very peculiar points about this case," he added. "As a matter of fact, I don't believe that Radnor Gaylord is any more guilty of the crime than I am—or I shouldn't have come. But it won't do for me to jump at conclusions until I get more data. I suppose you realize what is the peculiarly significant point about the murder?"

"You mean Mose's disappearance?"

"Well, no. I didn't have that in mind. That's significant enough to be sure, but nothing but what you would naturally expect. The crime was committed, if your data is straight, either by him or in his presence, and of course he disappears. You could scarcely have expected to find him sitting there waiting for you, in either case."

"You mean Radnor's behavior on the day of the murder and his refusal to explain it?" I asked uneasily.

"No," Terry laughed. "That may be significant and it may not—I strongly suspect that it is not. What I mean, is the peculiar place in which the crime was committed. No person on earth could have foreseen that Colonel Gaylord would go alone into that cave. There is an accidental element about the murder. It must have been committed on the spur of the moment by someone who had not premeditated it—at least at that time. This is the point we must keep in mind."

He sat for a few moments staring at the dashboard with a puzzled frown.

"Broadly speaking," he said slowly, "I have found that you can place the motive of every wilful murder under one of three heads—avarice, fear or revenge. Suppose we consider the first. Could avarice have been the motive for Colonel Gaylord's murder? The body had not been robbed, you tell me?"

"No, we found a gold watch and considerable money in the pockets."

"Then, you see, if the motive were avarice, it could not have been immediate gain. That throws out the possibility that the murderer was some unknown thief who merely took advantage of a chance opportunity. If we are to conceive of avarice as the motive, the crime must have been committed by some person who would benefit more remotely by the Colonel's death. Did anyone owe him money that you know of?"

"There is no record of anything of the sort and he was a careful business man. I do not think he would have loaned money without making some memorandum of it. He held several mortgages but they, of course, revert to his heirs."

"I understood that Radnor was the only heir."

"He is, practically. There are a few minor bequests to the servants and to some old friends."

"Did the servants know that anything was to go to them?"

"No, I don't think they did."

"And this Cat-Eye Mose, did he receive a share?"

"Yes, larger than any of the others."

"It seems that Colonel Gaylord, at least, had confidence in him. And how about the other son? Did he know that he was to be disinherited?"

"I think that the Colonel made it plain at the time they parted."

Terry shook his head and frowned.

"This disinheriting business is bad. I don't like it and I never shall. It stirs up more ill-feeling than anything I know of. Jeff seems to have proved an alibi, however, and we will dismiss him for the present."

"Rad has always sympathized with Jeff," I said.

"Then," continued Terry, "if the servants did not know the contents of the will, and we have all of the data, Radnor is the only one who could knowingly have benefited by the Colonel's death. Suppose we take a glance at motives of fear. Do you know of anyone who had reason to stand in fear of the Colonel? He wasn't oppressing anybody? No damaging evidence against any person in his possession? Not levying blackmail was he?"

"Not that I know of," and I smiled slightly.

"It's not likely," mused Terry, "but you never can tell what is going to come out when a respectable man is dead.—And now as to revenge. With a man of Colonel Gaylord's character, there were likely to be a good many people who owed him a bad turn. He seems to have been a peppery old gentleman. It's quite on the cards that he had some enemies among his neighbors?"

"No, so far as I can discover, he was very popular in the neighborhood. The indignation over his death was something tremendous. When it first got out that Rad was accused of the crime, there was even talk of lynching him."

"So?—Servants all appeared to be fond of him?"

"The old family servants were broken-hearted at the news of his death. They had been, for the most part, born and bred on the place, and in spite of his occasional harshness they loved the Colonel with the old-fashioned devotion of the slave toward his master. He was in his way exceedingly kind to them. When old Uncle Eben died my uncle watched all night by his bed."

"It's a queer situation," Terry muttered, and relapsed into silence till we reached the jail.

It was an ivy-covered brick building set back from the street and shaded by trees.

"Rather more home-like than the Tombs," Terry commented. "Shouldn't mind taking a rest in it myself."

We found Radnor pacing up and down the small room in

which he was confined, like a caged animal; the anxiety and seclusion were beginning to tell on his nerves. He faced about quickly as the door opened and at sight of me his face lightened. He was growing pathetically pleased at having anyone with whom he could talk.

"Rad," I said with an air of cheerfulness which was not entirely assumed, "I hope we're nearing the end of our trouble at last. This is Mr. Patten—Terry Patten of New York, who has come to help me unravel the mystery."

It was an unfortunate beginning; I had told him before of Terry's connection with the Patterson-Pratt affair. He had half held out his hand as I commenced to speak, but he dropped it now with a slight frown.

"I don't think I care to be interviewed," he remarked curtly. "I have nothing to say for the benefit of the Post-Dispatch."

"You'd better," said Terry, imperturbably. "The Post-Dispatch prints the truth, you know, and some of the other papers don't. The truth's always the best in the end. I merely want to find out what information you can give me in regard to the ghost."

"I will tell you nothing," Radnor growled. "I am not giving statements to the press."

"Mr. Gaylord," said Terry, with an assumption of gentle patience, "if you will excuse my referring to what I know must be a painful subject, would you mind telling me if the suspicion has ever crossed your mind that your brother Jefferson may have returned secretly, have abstracted the bonds from the safe, and, two weeks later, quite accidentally, have met Colonel Gaylord alone in the cave—"

Radnor turned upon him in a sudden fury; I thought for a moment he was going to strike him and I sprang forward and caught his arm.

"The Gaylords may be a bad lot but they are not liars and they are not cowards. They do not run away; they stand by the consequences of their acts."

Terry bowed gravely.

"Just one more question, and I am through. What happened to you that day in the cave?"

"It's none of your damned business!"

I glanced apprehensively at Terry, uncertain as to how he would take this; but he did not appear to resent it. He looked Radnor over with an air of interested approval and his smile slowly broadened.

"I'm glad to see you're game," he remarked.

"I tell you I don't know who killed my father any more than you do," Radnor cried. "You needn't come here asking me questions. Go and find the murderer if you can, and if you can't, hang me and be done with it."

"I don't know that we need take up any more of Mr. Gaylord's time," said Terry to me. "I've found out about all I wished to know. We'll drop in again," he added reassuringly to Radnor. "Good afternoon."

As we went out of the door he turned back a moment and added with a slightly sharp undertone in his voice:

"And the next time I come, Gaylord, you'll shake hands!" Fumbling in his pocket he drew out my telegram from the police commissioner, and tossed it onto the cot. "In the meantime there's something for you to think about. Good by."

"Do you mean," I asked as we climbed back into the carriage, "that Radnor did believe Jeff guilty?"

"Well, not exactly. I fancy he will be relieved, though, to find that Jeff was three thousand miles away when the murder was committed."

Only once during the drive home did Terry exhibit any interest in his surroundings, and that was when we passed through the village of Lambert Corners. He made me slow down to a walk and explain the purpose of everyone of the dozen or so buildings along the square. At "Miller's place" he suddenly decided that he needed some stamps and I waited outside while he obtained them together with a drink in the private back room.

"Nothing like getting the lay of the land," he remarked as he climbed back into the carriage. "That Miller is a picturesque old party. He thinks it's all tommy-rot that Radnor Gaylord had anything to do with the crime—Rad's a customer of his, and it's a downright imposition to lock the boy up where he can't spend money."

For the rest of the drive Terry kept silence and I did not venture to interrupt it. I had come to have a superstitious feeling that his silences were portentous. It was not until I stopped to open the gate into our own home lane, that he suddenly burst out with the question:

"Where do the Mathers people live?"

"A couple of miles farther down the pike—they have no connection whatever with the business, and don't know a thing about it."

"Ah—perhaps not. Would it be too late to drive over to-night?"

"Yes," said I, "it would."

"Oh, very well," said he, good-humoredly. "There'll be time enough in the morning."

I let this pass without comment, but on one thing I was resolved; and that was that Polly Mathers should never fall into Terry's clutches.

"There are a lot of questions I want to ask about your ghost, but I'll wait till I get my bearings—and my dinner," he added with a laugh. "There wasn't any dining car on that train, and I breakfasted early and omitted lunch."

"Here we are," I said, as we came in sight of the house. "The cook is expecting us."

"So that is the Gaylord house is it? A fine old place! When was it built?"

"About 1830, I imagine."

"Let me see, Sheridan rode up the Shenandoah Valley and burned everything in sight. How did this place happen to escape?"

"I don't know just how it did. You see it's a mile back from the main road and well hidden by trees—I suppose they were in a hurry and it escaped their attention."

"And that row of shanties down there?"

"Are the haunted negro cabins."

"Ah!" Terry rose in his seat and scanned them eagerly. "We'll have a look at them as soon as I get something to eat. Really, a farm isn't so bad," he remarked as he stepped out upon the portico. "And is this Solomon?" he inquired as the old negro came forward to take his bag. "Well, Solomon, I've been reading about you in the papers! You and I are going to have a talk by and by."

CHAPTER XVII

WE SEARCH THE ABANDONED CABINS

"Now," said Terry, as Solomon and the suitcase disappeared upstairs, "let's you and I have a look at those haunted cabins."

"I thought you were hungry!"

"Starving—but I still have strength enough to get that far. Solomon says supper won't be ready for half an hour, and we haven't half an hour to waste. I'm due in the city the day after to-morrow, remember."

"You won't find anything," I said. "I've searched every one of those cabins myself and the ha'nt didn't leave a trace behind him."

"I think I'll just glance about with my own eyes," laughed Terry. "Reporters sometimes see things, you know, where corporation lawyers don't."

"Just as you please," I replied. "Four-Pools is at your disposal."

I led the way across the lawn and into the laurel growth. Terry followed with eyes eagerly alert; the gruesome possibilities of the place appealed to him. He pushed through the briars that surrounded the first cabin and came out on the slope behind, where he stood gazing down delightedly at the dark waters of the fourth pool.

"My word! This is great. We'll run a half-page picture and call it the 'Haunted Tarn.' Didn't know such places really existed—thought writers made 'em up. Come on," he called, plunging back to the laurel walk, "we must catch our ghost; I don't want this scenery to go to waste."

We commenced at the first cabin and went down the row thoroughly and systematically. At Terry's insistence one of the stable men brought a ladder and we climbed into every loft, finding nothing but spiders and dust. The last on the left, being more weatherproof than the others, was used as a granary. A space six feet square was left inside the door, but for the rest the room was filled nearly to the ceiling with sacks of Indian meal.

"How about this—did you examine this cabin?"

"Well, really, Terry; there isn't much room for a ghost here."

"Ghosts don't require much room; how about the loft?"

"I didn't go up—you can't get at the trap without moving all the meal."

"I see!" Terry was examining the three walls of sacks before us. "Now here is a sack rather dirtier than the rest and squashy. It looks to me as if it had had a good deal of rough handling."

He pulled it to the floor as he spoke, and another with it. A space some three feet high was visible; by crawling one could make his way along without hitting the ceiling.

"Come on!" said Terry, scrambling to the top of the pile and pulling me after him, "we've struck the trail of our ghostly friend unless I'm very much mistaken.—Look at that!" He pointed to a muddy foot-mark plainly outlined on one of the sacks. "Don't disturb it; we may want to compare it with the marks in the cave.—Hello! What's this? The print of a bare foot—that's our friend, Mose."

He took out a pocket rule and made careful measurements of both prints; the result he set down in a note book. I was quite as excited now as Terry. We crawled along on all fours until we reached the open trap; there was no trace here of either spider-webs or dust. We scrambled into the loft without much difficulty, and found a large room with sloping beams overhead and two small windows, innocent of glass, at either end. The room was empty but clean; it had been thoroughly swept, and recently. Terry poked about but found nothing.

"H'm!" he grunted. "Mose cleaned well.—Ah! Here we are!"

He paused before a horizontal beam along the side wall and pointed to a little pile of ashes and a cigar stub.

"He smokes cigars, and good strong ones—at least he isn't a lady. Did you ever see a cigar like that before?"

"Yes," I said, "that's the kind the Colonel always smoked—a fresh box was stolen from the dining-room cupboard a day or so after I got here. Solomon said it was the ha'nt, but we suspected it was Solomon."

"Was the cupboard unlocked?"

"Oh, yes; any of the house servants could have got at it."

"Well," said Terry, poking his head from the windows for a view of the ground beneath, "that's all there seems to be here; we might as well go down."

We boosted up the two meal bags again, and started back toward the house. Terry's eyes studied his surroundings keenly, whether for the sake of the story he was planning to write or the mystery he was trying to solve, I could only conjecture. His glance presently fixed on the stables where old Uncle Jake was visible sitting on an upturned pail in the doorway.

"You go on," he ordered, "and have 'em put dinner or supper or whatever you call it on the table, and I'll be back in three minutes. I want to see what that old fellow over there has to say in regard to the ghost."

It was fifteen minutes later that Terry reappeared.

"Well," I inquired as I led the way to the dining-room, "did you get any news of the ghost?"

"Did I! The Society for Psychical Research ought to investigate this neighborhood. They'd find more spirits in half an hour than they've found in their whole past history."

Terry's attention during supper was chiefly directed toward Nancy's fried chicken and beat biscuits. When he did make any remarks he addressed them to Solomon rather than to me. Solomon was loquacious enough in general, but he had his own ideas of table decorum, and it was evident that the friendly advances of my guest considerably scandalized him. When the coffee and cigars were brought on, Terry appeared to be on the point of inviting Solomon to sit down and have a cigar with us;

but he thought better of it, and contented himself with talking to the old man across my shoulder. He confined his questions to matters concerning the household and the farm, and Solomon in vain endeavored to confine his replies to "yes, sah," "no, sah," "jes' so, sah!" In five minutes he was well started, and it would have required a flood-gate to stop him.

In the midst of it Terry rose and dismissing me with a brief, "I'll join you in the library later; I want to talk to Solomon a few minutes," he bowed me out and shut the door.

I was amused rather than annoyed by this summary dismissal. Terry had been in the house not quite two hours, and I am sure that a third person, looking on, would have picked me out for the stranger. Terry's way of being at home in any surroundings was absolutely inimitable. Had he ever had occasion to visit Windsor Castle I am sure that he would have set about immediately making King Edward feel at home.

He appeared in the library in the course of half an hour with the apology: "I hope you didn't mind being turned out. Servants are sometimes embarrassed, you know, about telling the truth before any of the family."

"You didn't get much truth out of Solomon," I retorted.

"I don't know that I did," Terry admitted with a laugh. "There are the elements of a good reporter in Solomon; he has an imagination which I respect. The Gaylords appear to be an interesting family with hereditary tempers. The ghost, I hear, beat a slave to death, and to pay for it is doomed to pace the laurel walk till the day of judgment."

"That's the story," I nodded, "and the beating is at least authentic."

"H'm!" Terry frowned. "And Solomon tells me tales of the Colonel himself whipping the negroes—there can't be any truth in that?"

"But there is," I said. "He didn't hesitate to strike them when he was angry. I myself saw him beat a nigger a few days ago," and I recounted the story of the chicken thief.

"So! A man of that sort is likely to have enemies he doesn't suspect. How about Cat-Eye Mose? Was Colonel Gaylord in the habit of whipping him?"

"Often," I nodded, "but the more the Colonel abused Mose, the fonder Mose appeared to grow of the Colonel."

"It's a puzzling situation," said Terry pacing up and down the room with a thoughtful frown. "Well!" he exclaimed with a sudden access of energy, "I suppose we might as well sit down and tackle it."

He took off his coat and rolled up his shirt sleeves; then shoving everything back from one end of the big library table, he settled himself in a chair and motioned me to one opposite.

"Tomorrow morning," he said as he took out from his pockets a roll of newspaper clippings and a yellow copy pad, "we will drive over and have a look at that cave; it ought to tell its own story. But in the meantime—" he looked up with a laugh—"suppose we use our brains a little."

I did not resent the inference. Terry was his old impudent self, and I was so relieved at having him there, assuming the responsibility, that he might have wiped the floor with me and welcome.

"Our object," he commenced, "is not to prove your cousin innocent of the murder, but to find out who is guilty. The most logical method would be to study the scene of the crime first, but as that does not appear feasible until morning, we will examine such data as we have. On the face of it the only two who appear to be implicated are Radnor and this Cat-Eye Mose—who is a most picturesque character," Terry added, the reporter for the moment getting ahead of the detective.

He paused and examined the end of his fountain pen speculatively, and then ran through the pile of clippings before him.

"Well, now, as for Radnor. Suppose we look into his case a little." He glanced over one of the newspaper slips and tossed it across to me.

"There's a clipping from the 'Baltimore Censor'—a tolerably conservative journal. What have you to say in regard to it?"

I picked it up and glanced it over. It was dated May twenty-third—four days after the murder—and was the same in substance as many other articles I had read in the past week.

"No new evidence has come to light in regard to the sensational murder of Colonel Gaylord whose body was discovered in Luray Cave, Virginia, a few days ago. The authorities now concur in the belief that the crime was committed by the son of the murdered man. The accused is awaiting trial in the Kennisburg jail.

"It seems impossible that any man, however depraved, could in cold blood commit so brutal and unnatural a crime as that with which Radnor Gaylord is accused. It is only in the light of his past history that the action can be understood. Coming from one of the oldest families of Virginia, an heir to wealth and an honored name, he is but another example of the many who have sold their birth-right for a mess of pottage. A drunkard and a spendthrift, he wasted his youth in gambling and betting on the races while honest men were toiling for their daily bread.

"Several times has Radnor Gaylord been disinherited and turned adrift, but Colonel Gaylord, weak in his love for his youngest son, invariably received him back again into the house he had dishonored. Finally, pressed beyond the point of endurance, the old man took a firm stand and refused to meet his son's inordinate demands for money. Young Gaylord, rendered desperate by debts, took the most obvious method of gaining his inheritance. His part in the tragedy of Colonel Gaylord's death is as good as proved, though he persistently and defiantly denies all knowledge of the crime. No sympathy can be felt for him. The wish of every right-minded man in the country must be that the law will take its course—and that as speedily as possible."

"Well?" said Terry as I finished.

"It's a lie," I cried hotly.

"All of it?"

"Every word of it!"

"Oh, see here," said Terry. "There's no use in your trying to hide things. That account is an exaggeration of course, but it must have some foundation. You told me you weren't afraid of the truth. Just be so kind as to tell it to me, then. Exactly what sort of a fellow is Radnor? I want to know for several reasons."

"Well, he did drink a good deal for a youngster," I admitted, "though never to such an extent as has been reported. Of late he had stopped entirely. As for gambling, the young men around here have got into a bad way of playing for high stakes, but during the past month or so Rad had pulled up in that too. He sometimes backed one of their own horses from the Gaylord stables, but so did the Colonel; it's the regular thing in Virginia. As for his ever having been disinherited, that is a newspaper story, pure and simple. I never heard anything of the sort, and the neighborhood has told me pretty much all there is to know within the last few days."

"His father never turned him out of the house then?"

"Never that I heard of. He did leave home once because his father insulted him, but he came back again."

"That was forgiving," commented Terry. "In general, though, I understand that the relations between the two were rather strained?"

"At times they were," I admitted, "but things had been going rather better for the last few days."

"Until the night before the murder. They quarreled then? And over a matter of money?"

"Yes. Radnor makes no secret of it. He wanted his father to settle something on him, and upon his father's refusal some words passed between them."

"And a French clock," suggested Terry.

I acknowledged the clock and Terry pondered the question with one eye closed meditatively.

"Had Radnor ever asked for anything of the sort before?"

"Not that I know of."

"Why did he ask then?"

"Well, it's rather galling for a man of his age to be dependent on his father for every cent he gets. The Colonel always gave him plenty, but he did not want to take it in that way."

"In just what way did he want to take it?" Terry inquired. "Since he was so infernally independent why didn't he get to work and earn something?"

"Earn something!" I returned sharply. "Rad has managed the whole plantation for the last three years. His father was getting too old for business and if Rad hadn't taken hold, things would have gone to the deuce long ago. All he got as a regular salary was fifty dollars a month; I think it was time he was paid for his services."

"Oh, very well," Terry laughed. "I was merely asking the question. And if you will allow me to go a step further, why did Colonel Gaylord object to settling something on the boy?"

"He wanted to keep him under his thumb. The Colonel liked to rule, and he wished everyone around him to be dependent on his will."

"I see!" said Terry. "Radnor had a real grievance, then, after all—just one thing more on this point. Why did he choose that particular time to make his request? You say he has had practical charge of affairs for the past three years. Why did he not wish to be independent last year? Or why did he not postpone the desire until next year?"

I shrugged my shoulders.

"You'll have to ask Radnor that." I had my own suspicions, but I did not wish to drag Polly Mathers's name into the discussion.

Terry watched me a moment without saying anything, and then he too shrugged his shoulders as he turned back to the newspaper clippings.

"I won't go into the matter of Radnor's connection with the ha'nt just now; I should like to consider first his actions on the day of the murder. I have here a report of the testimony taken at the inquest, but it is not so full as I could wish in some particulars. I should like to have you give me the details. First, you say that Radnor and his father did not speak at the breakfast table? How was it when you started?"

"They both appeared to be in pretty good spirits, but I noticed that they avoided each other."

"Very well, tell me exactly what you did after you arrived at Luray."

"We left our horses at the hotel and walked about a mile across the fields to the mouth of the cave. We had lunch in the woods and at about one o'clock we started through the cave. We came out at a little after three, and, I should say, started to drive back about half past four."

"Did you notice Radnor through the day?"

"Not particularly."

"Did you see either him or the Colonel in the cave?"

"Yes, I was with the Colonel most of the time."

"And how about Radnor? Didn't you see him at all?"

"Oh, yes. I remember talking to him once about some queerly shaped stalagmites. He didn't hang around me, naturally, while I was with his father."

"And when you talked to him about the stalagmites—was there anyone else with him at the time?"

"I believe Miss Mathers was there."

"And he was carrying her coat?"

"I didn't notice."

"At least he left it later in what you call the gallery of the broken column?"

"Yes."

"I see," said Terry glancing over the printed report of the inquest, "that the coroner asked at this point if Radnor were in the habit of forgetting young ladies' coats. That's more pertinent than many of the questions he asked. How about it? Was he in the habit of forgetting young ladies' coats?"

"I really don't know, Terry," I said somewhat testily.

"It's a pity you're not more observing," he returned, "for it's important, on the whole. But never mind. I'll find that out for myself. Did you notice when he left the rest of the party?"

"No, there was such a crowd of us that I didn't miss him."

"Very well, we'll have a look at his testimony. He left the rest of you in this same gallery of the broken column, went straight out, strolled about the woods for half an hour or so and then returned to the hotel. I fancy 'strolled' is not precisely the right word, but at any rate it's the word he uses. Now that half hour in the woods is an unfortunate circumstance. Had he gone directly to the hotel from the cave, we could have proved an alibi without any difficulty. As it is, he had plenty of time after the others came out to remember that he had forgotten the coat, return for it, renew the quarrel with his father, and after the fatal result make his way to the hotel while the rest of the party were still loitering in the woods."

"Terry—" I began.

He waved his hand in a gesture of dissent.

"Oh, I'm not saying that's what *did* happen. I'm just showing you that the district attorney's theory is a physical possibility. Let's glance at the landlord's testimony a moment. When Radnor returned for his horse he appeared angry, excited and in a hurry. Those are the landlord's words, and they are corroborated by the stable boy and several loungers about the hotel.

"He was in a hurry—why? Because he wished to get away before the others came back. He had suddenly decided while he was in the woods—probably when he heard them laughing and talking as they came out of the cave—that he did not wish to see anyone. He was angry—mark that. All of the witnesses agree there, and I think that his actions carry out their evidence. He drank two glasses of brandy—by the way, I understood you to say he had stopped drinking. He ordered the stable boy about sharply. He swore at him for being slow. He lashed his horse quite unnecessarily as he galloped off. He rode home at an outrageous rate. And he was not, Solomon gives me to understand, in the habit of maltreating horses.

"Now what do you make of all this? Here is a young man with an unexpended lot of temper on his hands—bent on being reckless; bent on being just as bad as he can be. It's as clear as daylight. That boy never committed any crime. A man who had just murdered his father would not be filled with anger, no matter what the provocation had been. He might be overcome with horror, fear, remorse—a dozen different emotions, but anger would not be among them. And further, a man who had committed a crime and intended to deny it later, would not proclaim his feelings in quite that blatant manner. Young Gaylord had not injured anyone; he himself had been injured. He was mad through and through, and he didn't care who knew it. He expended—you will remember—the most of his belligerency on his horse on the way home, and you found him in the summer house undergoing the natural reaction. By evening he had got himself well in hand again and was probably considerably ashamed of his conduct. He doesn't care to talk about the matter for several reasons. Fortunately Solomon is not so scrupulous."

"I don't know what you're driving at, Terry," said I.

"Don't you?" he inquired. "Well, really, it's about time that I came down!" He paused while he scrawled one or two sentences on his copy pad, then he glanced up with a laugh. "I don't know myself, but I think I can make a pretty good guess. We'll call on Miss Polly Mathers in the morning and see if she can't help us out."

"Terry," I expostulated, "that girl knows no more about the matter than I do. She has already given her testimony, and I positively will not have her name mentioned in connection with the affair."

"I don't see how you can help it," was his cool reply. "If she's in, she's in, and I'm not to blame. However, we won't quarrel about it now; we'll pay her a call in the morning." He ran his eyes over the clippings again, then added, "There are just two more points connecting Radnor Gaylord with the murder that need explaining: the foot-prints in the cave and the match box. The foot-prints I will dismiss for the present because I have not seen them myself and I can't make any deductions from hearsay evidence. But the question of the match box may repay a little investigation. I want you to tell me precisely what happened in the woods before you went into the cave. In the first place, how many older people were there in the party?"

"Mr. and Mrs. Mathers, a lady who was visiting them and Colonel Gaylord."

"There were two servants, I understand, besides this Mose, to help about the lunch. What did they do?"

"Well, I don't know exactly. I wasn't paying much attention. I believe they carried things over from the hotel, collected wood for the fire, and then went to a farm house for water."

"But Mrs. Mathers, it seems, attended to lighting the fire?"

"Yes, she and the Colonel made the fire and started the coffee."

"Ah!" said Terry with a note of satisfaction in his voice. "The matter begins to clear. Was Colonel Gaylord in the habit of smoking?"

"He smoked one cigar after every meal."

"Never any more than that?"

"No, the doctor had limited him. The Colonel grumbled about it regularly, and always smoked the biggest blackest cigar he could find."

"And where did he get his matches?"

"Solomon passed the brass match box from the dining-room mantelpiece just as he passed it to us to-night."

"Colonel Gaylord was not in the habit of carrying matches in his pockets then?"

"No, I think not."

"We may safely assume," said Terry, "that in this matter of making the fire, if the two were working together, the Colonel was on his knees arranging the sticks while Mrs. Mathers was standing by, giving directions. That, I believe, is the usual division of labor. Well, then, they get to the point of needing a light. The Colonel feels through his pockets, finds that he hasn't a match and—what happens?"

"What did happen," I broke in, "was that Mrs. Mathers turned to a group of us who were standing talking at one side, and asked if any of us had a match, and Rad handed her his box. That is the last anyone remembers about it."

"Exactly!" said Terry. "And I think I can tell you the rest. You can see for yourself what took place. Mrs. Mathers went back to the spot where they were building the fire, and the Colonel took the match box from her. No man is ever going to stand by and watch a woman strike a match—he can do it so much better himself. At this point, Mrs. Mathers—by her own testimony—was called away, and she doesn't remember anything further about the box. She thinks that she returned it. Why? For no reason on earth except that she usually returns things. As a matter of fact, however, she didn't do it this time. She was called away and the Colonel was left to light the fire alone. He recognized the box as his son's and he dropped it into his pocket. At another time perhaps he would have walked over and handed it back; but not then. The two were not speaking to each other. Later, at the time of the struggle in the cave, the box fell from the old man's pocket, and formed a most damaging piece of circumstantial evidence against his son.

"On the whole," Terry finished, "I do not think we shall have a very difficult time in clearing Radnor. I had arrived at my own conclusions concerning him from reading the papers; what extra data I needed, I managed to glean from Solomon's lies. And as for you," he added, gazing across at me with an imperturbable grin, "I think you were wise in deciding to be a corporation lawyer."

CHAPTER XVIII

TERRY ARRIVES AT A CONCLUSION

"And now," said Terry, lighting a fresh cigar, and after a few preliminary puffs, settling down to work again, "we will consider the case of Cat-Eye Mose—a beautiful name, by the way, and apparently a beautiful character. It won't be my fault if we don't make a beautiful story out of him. You, yourself, I believe, hold the opinion that he committed the murder?"

"I am sure of it," I cried.

"In that case," laughed Terry, "I should be inclined to think him innocent."

I shrugged my shoulders. There was nothing to be gained by getting angry. If Terry chose to regard the solving of a murder mystery in the light of a joke, I had nothing to say; though I did think he might have realized that to me, at least, it was a serious matter.

"And you base your suspicions, do you not, upon the fact that he has queer eyes?"

"Not entirely."

"Upon what then?"

"Upon the fact that he took part in the struggle which ended in my uncle's death."

"Well, certainly, that does seem rather conclusive—there is no mistake about the foot-prints?"

"None whatever; the Mathers niggers both wore shoes, and anyway they didn't go into the cave."

"In that case I suppose it's fair to assume that Mose took part in the struggle. Whether he was the only man or whether there was still a third, the cave itself ought to tell a pretty clear story."

Terry rose and paced up and down the room once or twice, and then came back and picked up one of the newspaper clippings.

"It says here that the boot marks of two different men are visible."

"That's the sheriff's opinion," I replied. "Though I myself, can't make out anything but the marks of Mose and the Colonel. I examined everything carefully, but it's awfully mixed up, you know. One really can't tell much about it."

Terry impatiently flung himself into the chair again.

"I ought to have come down last week! If I had supposed you people could muddle matters up so thoroughly I should. I dare say you've trampled the whole place over till there isn't one of the original marks left."

"Look here, Terry," I said. "You act as if Virginia belonged to you. We've all been working our heads off over this business, and you come in at the last moment and quarrel with our data. You can go over tomorrow morning and collect your own evidence if you think it's so far superior to anyone else's. The marks are just as they were. Boards have been laid over them and nothing's been disturbed."

"You're rather done up, old man," Terry remarked, smiling across at me good-humoredly. "Of course it's quite on the cards that Cat-Eye Mose committed the crime—but there are a number of objections. As I understand it, he has the reputation of being a harmless, peaceable fellow not very bright but always good-natured. He never resented an injury, was never known to quarrel with anyone, took what was given him and said thank you. He loved Colonel Gaylord and watched over his interests as jealously as a dog. Well now, is a man who has had this reputation all his life, a man whom everybody trusts, very likely to go off the hook as suddenly as that and—with no conceivable motive—brutally kill the master he has served so faithfully? A man's future is in a large measure determined by his past."

"That may all be true enough," I said, "but it is very possible that people were deceived in Mose. I have been suspicious of him from the moment I laid eyes on him. You may think it unfair to judge a man from his physical appearance, but I wish you could once see Cat-Eye Mose yourself, and you would know what I mean. The people around here are used to him and don't notice it so much, but his eyes are yellow—positively yellow, and they narrow in the light just like a cat's. One night he drove Radnor and me home from a party, and I could actually see his eyes shining in the dark. It's the most gruesome thing I ever saw; and take that on top of his habits—he carries snakes around in the front of his shirt—really, one suspects him of anything."

"I hope he isn't dead," Terry murmured wistfully. "I'd like a personal interview."

He sat sunk down in his chair for several minutes intently examining the end of his fountain pen.

"Well," he said rousing himself, "it's time we had a shy at the ghost. We must find out in what way Radnor and Mose were connected with him, and in what way he was connected with the robbery. Radnor could help us considerably if he would only talk—the fact that he won't talk is very suggestive. We'll get at the truth without him, though. Suppose you begin and tell me everything from the first appearance of the ha'nt. I should like to get him tabulated."

"The first definite thing that reached the house," I replied, "was the night of my arrival when the roast chicken was stolen—I've told you that in detail."

"And it was that same night that Aunt What-Ever-Her-Name-Is saw the ghost in the laurel walk?"

I nodded.

"Did she say what it looked like?"

"It was white."

"And when you searched the cabins did you go into the one where the grain is stored?"

"No, Mose dropped his torch at the entrance. And anyway Rad said there was no use in searching it; it was already full to the brim with sacks of corn meal."

"Do you think that Radnor was trying to divert you from the scene?"

"No, I am sure he hadn't a suspicion himself."

"And what did the thing look like that you saw Mose carrying to the cabins in the night?"

"It seemed to be a large black bundle. I have thought since that it might have been clothes or blankets or something of that sort."

"So much for the first night," said Terry. "Now, how soon did the ghost appear again?"

"Various things were stolen after that, and the servants attributed it to the ha'nt, but the first direct knowledge I had was the night of the party when Radnor acted so strangely. I told you of his going back in the night."

"He was carrying something too?"

"Yes, he had a black bundle—it might have been clothes."

"And after that he and Mose were in constant consultation?"

"Yes—they both encouraged the belief in the ha'nt among the negroes and did their best to keep everyone away from the laurel walk. I overheard Mose several times telling stories to the other negroes about the terrible things the ha'nt would do if it caught them."

"And he himself didn't show any fear over the stories?"

"Not the slightest—appeared rather to enjoy them."

"And Radnor—how did he take the matter?"

"He was moody and irritable. I could see that something was preying on his mind."

"How did you explain the matter to yourself?"

"I was afraid he had fallen into the clutches of someone who was threatening him, possibly levying blackmail."

"But you didn't make any attempt to discover the truth?"

"Well, it was Rad's own affair, and I didn't want the appearance of spying. I did keep my eyes open as much as I could."

"And the Colonel, how did he take all this excitement about the ha'nt?"

"It bothered him considerably, but Rad kept him from hearing it as much as he could."

"When did the ha'nt appear again after the party?"

"Oh, by that time all sorts of rumors were running about among the negroes. The whole place was haunted and several of the plantation hands had left. But the next thing that we heard directly was in the early evening before the robbery when Mose, appearing terribly frightened, said he had seen the ha'nt rising in a cloud of blue smoke out of the spring-hole."

"And how did the Colonel and Radnor take this?"

"The Colonel was angry because he had been bragging about Mose not being afraid, and Rad was dazed. He didn't know what to think; he hustled Mose out of the way before we could ask any questions."

"And what did you think?"

"Well, I fancied at the time that he had really seen something, but as I thought it over in the light of later events I came to the conclusion that he was shamming, both then and in the middle of the night when he roused the house."

"That is, you wished to think him shamming, in order to prove his complicity in the robbery and the murder; and so you twisted the facts to suit your theory?"

"I don't think you can say that," I returned somewhat hotly. "It's merely a question of interpreting the facts."

"He didn't gain much by raising all that hullabaloo in the middle of the night."

"Why yes, that was done in order to throw suspicion on the ha'nt."

"Oh, I see!" laughed Terry. "Well, now, let's get to the end of this matter. Was any more seen of the ha'nt after that night?"

"No, at least not directly. For five or six days everyone was so taken up with the robbery that the ha'nt excitement rather died down. Then I believe there were some rumors among the negroes but nothing much reached the house."

"And since the murder nothing whatever has been seen

of the ha'nt?"

I shook my head.

"Just give me a list of the things that were stolen."

"Well, the roast chicken, a box of cigars, some shirts off the line, a suit of Rad's pajamas, a French novel, some brandy, quite a lot of things to eat—fresh loaves of bread, preserves, a boiled ham, sugar, coffee—oh, any amount of stuff! The niggers simply helped themselves and laid it to the ha'nt. One of the carriages was left out one night, and in the morning the cushions were gone and two lap robes. At the same time a water pail was taken and a pair of Jake's overalls. And then to end up came the robbery of the safe."

"The ha'nt had catholic tastes. Any of the things turned up since?"

"Yes, a number of things, such as blankets and clothes and dishes have gradually drifted back."

"The carriage cushions and lap robes—ever find them?"

"Never a trace—and why anyone should want 'em, I don't know!"

"What color were the lap robes?"

"Plain black broadcloth."

Terry got up and paced about a few moments and then came back and sat down.

"One thing is clear," he said, "there are two ha'nts."

"Two ha'nts! What do you mean?"

"Just what I say. Suppose for convenience we call them ha'nt number one, and ha'nt number two. Number one occupied apartments over the grain bin and haunted the laurel walk. He was white—I don't wonder at that if he spent much time crawling over those flour sacks. He smoked cigars and read French novels; Mose waited on him and Radnor knew about him—and didn't get much enjoyment out of the knowledge. It took money to get rid of him—a hundred dollars down and the promise of more to come. Radnor himself drove him off in the carriage the night he left, and Mose obliterated all traces of his presence. So much for number one.

"As for number two, he appeared three or four days before the robbery and haunted pretty much the whole place, especially the region of the spring-hole. In appearance he was nine feet tall, transparent, and black. Smoke came from his mouth and blue flames from his eyes. There was a sulphurous odor about him. He was first seen rising out of the spring-hole, and there is a passage in the bottom of the spring-hole that leads straight down to hell. Solomon is my authority.

"I asked him how he explained the apparition and he reckoned it was the ghost of the slave who was beaten to death, and that since his old master had come back to haunt the laurel walk, he had come back to haunt his old master. That sounds to me like a plausible explanation. As soon as it's light I'll have a look at the spring-hole."

"Terry," I said disgustedly, "that may make a very picturesque newspaper story, but it doesn't help much in unravelling the mystery."

"It helps a good deal. I would not like to swear to the flames or sulphur or the passage down to hell, but the fact that he was tall and black and comes from the spring-hole is significant. He was black—mark that—so were the stolen lap robes.

"Now you see how the matter stands on the night of the robbery. While ghost number one was out driving with Radnor, ghost number two entered the house through the open library window, found the safe ajar and helped himself. Let's consider what he took—five thousand dollars in government bonds, two deeds, an insurance policy, and a quart of small change—a very suggestive lot of loot if you think about it enough. After the robbery he disappeared, nothing seen of him for five or six days; then he turned up again for a day or so, and finally disappeared forever. So much for ha'nt number two. He's the party we're after. He pretty certainly robbed the safe and he possibly committed the murder—as to that I won't have any proof until I see the cave."

He stretched his arms with a laugh.

"Oh, this isn't so bad! All we've got to do now is to identify those two ghosts."

"I'm glad if you think it's so easy," I said somewhat sullenly. "But I will tell you one thing, if you go to basing any deductions on Solomon's stories you'll find yourself bumping against a stone wall."

"We'll have Rad over to dinner with us tomorrow night," Terry declared.

He rose and pulled out his watch.

"It's a quarter before ten. I think it's time you went to bed. You look about played out. You haven't been sleeping much of late?"

"No, I can't say that I have."

"I ought to have come down at once," said Terry, "but I'm always so blamed afraid of hurting people's feelings."

I stared slightly. I had never considered that one of Terry's weak points, but as he seemed to be quite in earnest, I let the remark pass.

"Do you think I could knock up one of the stable-men to drive me to the village? I know it's pretty late but I've got to send a couple of telegrams."

"Telegrams?" I demanded. "Where to?"

Terry laughed.

"Well, I must send a word to the Post-Dispatch to the effect that the Luray mystery grows more mysterious every hour. That the police have been wasting their energies on the wrong scent, but that the Post-Dispatch's special correspondent has arrived on the scene, and that we may accordingly look for a speedy solution."

"What is the second one?" I asked.

"To your friend, the police commissioner of Seattle."

"You don't think that Jeff—?"

"My dear fellow, I don't think, unless I have facts to think about.—Don't look so nervous; I'm not accusing him of anything. I merely want more details than you got; I'm a newspaper man, remember, and I like local color even in telegrams. And now, go to bed; and for heaven's sake, go to sleep. The case is in the hands of the Post-Dispatch's young man, and you needn't worry any more."

CHAPTER XIX

TERRY FINDS THE BONDS

I was wakened the next morning by Terry clumping into my room dressed in riding breeches and boots freshly spattered with mud.

They were Radnor's clothes—Terry had taken me at my word and was thoroughly at home.

"Hello, old man!" he said, sitting down on the edge of the bed. "Been asleep, haven't you? Sorry to wake you, but we've got a day's work ahead. Hope you don't mind my borrowing Radnor's togs. Didn't come down prepared for riding. Solomon gave 'em to me—seemed to think that Radnor wouldn't need 'em any more. Oh, Solomon and I are great friends!" he added with a laugh, as he suddenly appeared to remember the object of his visit and commenced a search through his pockets.

I sat up in bed and watched him impatiently. It was evident that he had some news, and equally evident that he was going to be as leisurely as possible about imparting it.

"This is a pretty country," he remarked as he finished with his coat pockets and commenced on the waistcoat. "It would be almost worth living in if many little affairs like this occurred to keep things going."

"Really, Terry," I said, "when you refer to my uncle's murder as a 'little affair' I think you're going too far!"

"Oh, I beg your pardon," he returned good-naturedly, "I guess I am incorrigible. I didn't know Colonel Gaylord personally, you see, and I'm so used to murders that I've come to think it's the only natural way of dying. Anyhow," he added, as he finally produced a yellow envelope, "I've got something here that will interest you. It explains why our young friend Radnor didn't want to talk."

He tossed the envelope on the bed and I eagerly tore out the telegram. It was from the police commissioner in Seattle and it ran:

"Jefferson Gaylord returned Seattle May fifth after absence six weeks. Said to have visited old home Virginia. Had been wanted by police. Suspected implication in case obtaining money false pretences. Mistaken charge. Case dismissed."

"What does it mean?" I asked.

"It means," said Terry, "that we've spotted ghost number one. It was clear from the first that Radnor was trying to shield someone, even at the expense of his own reputation. Leaving women out of the case, that pointed pretty straight toward his elder brother. Part of your theory was correct, the only trouble being that you carried it too far. You made Jeff commit both the robbery and the murder, while as a matter of fact he did neither. Then when you found a part of your theory was untenable you rejected the whole of it.

"This is how the matter stood: Jeff Gaylord was pretty desperately in need of money. I suspect that the charge against him, whatever it was, was true. The money he had taken had to be returned and somebody's silence bought before the thing could be hushed up. Anyway, Seattle was too hot to hold him and he lit out and came East. He applied to Radnor, but Radnor was in a tight place himself and couldn't lay his hands on anything except what his father had given him for a birthday present. That was tied up in another investment and if he converted it into cash it would be at a sacrifice. So it ran along for a week or so, while Rad was casting about for a means of getting his brother out of the way without any fresh scandal. But Mose's suddenly taking to seeing ha'nts precipitated matters. Realizing that his father's patience had reached its limit, and that he couldn't keep you off the scent much longer, he determined to borrow the money for Jeff's journey back to Seattle, and to close up his own investment.

"That same night he drove Jeff to the station at Kennisburg. The Washington express does not stop at Lambert Junction, and anyway Kennisburg is a bigger station and travellers excite less comment. This isn't deduction; it's fact. I rode to Kennisburg this morning and proved it. The station man remembers selling Radnor Gaylord a ticket to Washington in the middle of the night about three weeks ago. Some man who waited outside and whose face the agent did not see, boarded the train, and Rad drove off alone. The ticket seller does not know Rad personally but he knows him by sight—so much for that. Rad came home and went to bed. When he came down stairs in the morning he was met by the information that the ha'nt had robbed the safe. You can see what instantly jumped into his mind—some way, somehow, Jeff had taken those bonds—and yet figure on it as he might, he could not see how it was possible. The robbery seemed to have occurred while he was away. Could Jeff merely have pretended to leave? Might he have slipped off the train again and come back? Those are the questions that were bothering Radnor. He was honest in saying that he could not imagine how the bonds had been stolen, and yet he was also honest in not wanting to know the truth."

"He might have confided in me," I said.

"It would have been a good deal better if he had. But in order to understand Rad's point of view, you must take into account Jeff's character. He appears to have been a reckless, dashing, headstrong, but exceedingly attractive fellow. His father put up with his excesses for six years before the final quarrel. Cat-Eye Mose, so old Jake tells me, moped for months after his disappearance. Rad, as a little fellow, worshipped his bad but charming brother.—There you have it. Jeff turns up again with a hard luck story, and Mose and Radnor both go back to their old allegiance.

"Jeff is in a bad hole, a fugitive from justice with the penitentiary waiting for him. He confesses the whole thing to Radnor—extenuating circumstances plausibly to the fore. He has been dishonest, but unintentionally so. He wishes to straighten up and lead a respectable life. If he had, say fifteen hundred dollars, he could quash the indictment against him. He is Radnor's brother and the Colonel's son, but Rad is to receive a fortune while he is to be disinherited. The money he asks now is only his right. If he receives it he will disappear and trouble Rad no more.—That, I fancy, is the line of argument our returned prodigal used. Anyway, he won Rad over. Radnor was thinking of getting married, had plenty of use for all the money he could lay his hands on, but he seems to be a generous chap, and he sacrificed himself.

"For obvious reasons Jeff wished his presence kept a secret, and Rad and Mose respected his wishes. After the robbery Radnor was too sick at the thought that his brother may have betrayed him, to want to do anything but hush the matter up. At the news of the murder he did not know what to think; he would not believe Jeff guilty, and yet he did not see any other way out."

Terry paused a moment and leaned forward with an excited gleam in his eye.

"That," he said, "is the whole truth about ghost number one. Our business now is to track down number two, and here, as a starter are the missing bonds."

He tossed a pile of mildewed papers on the bed and met my astonishment with a triumphant chuckle.

It was true—all five of the missing bonds were there, the May first coupons still uncut. Also the deeds and insurance policy, exactly as they had left the safe, except that they were damp and mud-stained.

I stared for a moment too amazed to speak. Finally, "Where did you find them?" I gasped.

Terry regarded me with a tantalizing laugh.

"Exactly where I thought I'd find them. Oh, I've been out early this morning! I saw the sun rise, and breakfasted in Kennisburg at six forty-five. I'm ready for another breakfast though. Hurry up and dress. We've got a day's work before us. I'm off to the stables to talk 'horses' with Uncle Jake; when you're ready for breakfast send Solomon after me."

"Terry," I implored, "where on the face of the earth did you find those bonds?"

"At the mouth of the passage to hell," said Terry gravely, "but I'm not quite sure myself who put them there."

"Mose?" I queried eagerly.

"It might have been—and it might not." He waved his hand airily and withdrew.

CHAPTER XX

POLLY MAKES A CONFESSION

At breakfast Terry drank two cups of coffee and subsided into thought. I could get no more from him on the subject of the bonds; he was not sure himself, was all the satisfaction he would give. When the meal was half over, to Solomon's dismay, he suddenly rose without noticing a new dish of chicken livers that had just appeared at his elbow.

"Come on," he said impatiently, "you've had enough to eat. I've got to see those marks while they're still there. I'm desperately afraid an earthquake will swallow that cave before I get a chance at them."

Fifteen minutes later we were bowling down the lane behind the fastest pair of horses in the Gaylord stables, and through the prettiest country in the State of Virginia. Terry sat with his hands in his pockets and his eyes on the dash-board. As we came to the four corners at the valley-pike I reined in.

"Would you rather go the short way over the mountains by a very rough road, or the long way through Kennisburg?" I inquired.

"What's that?" he asked. "Oh, the short way by all means—but first I want to call at the Mathers's."

"It would simply be a waste of time."

"It won't take long—and since Radnor won't talk I've got to get at the facts from the other end. Besides, I want to see Polly myself."

"Miss Mathers knows nothing about the matter," said I as stiffly as possible.

"Doesn't she!" said Terry. "She knows a good many things, and it's about time she told them.—At any rate, you must admit that she's the owner of the unfortunate coat that caused the trouble; I want to ask her some questions about that. Why can't girls learn to carry their own coats? It would save a lot of trouble."

It ended by my driving, with a very bad grace, to Mathers Hall.

"You wait here until I come out," said Terry, coolly, as I drew up by the stepping stone and commenced fumbling for a hitching strap.

"Not much!" said I. "If you interview Polly Mathers I shall be present at the interview."

"Oh, very well!" he returned resignedly. "If you'd let me go about it my own way, though, I'd get twice as much out of her."

The family were at breakfast, the servant informed me. I left Terry in the parlor while I went on to the dining-room to explain the object of our visit.

"There is a friend of mine here from New York to help us about the trial"—I thought it best to suppress his real profession—"and he wants to interview Miss Polly in regard to the coat. I am very sorry—"

"Certainly," said Mrs. Mathers, "Polly is only too glad to help in any way possible."

And to my chagrin Polly excused herself and withdrew to the parlor, while her father kept me listening to a new and not very valuable theory of his in regard to the disappearance of Mose. It was fifteen minutes before I made my escape and knocked on the parlor door. I turned the knob and went in without waiting for a summons.

The Mathers's parlor is a long cool dim room with old-fashioned mahogany furniture and jars of roses scattered about. It was so dark after the bright sunshine of the rest of the house, that for a moment I didn't discover the occupants until the sound of Polly's sobbing proclaimed their whereabouts. I was somewhat taken aback to find her sitting in a corner of the big horsehair sofa, her head buried in the cushions, while Terry, nonchalantly leaning back in his chair, regarded her with much the expression that he might have worn at a "first night" at the theatre. It might also be noted that Polly wore a white dress with a big bunch of roses in her belt, that her hair was becomingly rumpled by the cushion, and that she was not crying hard enough to make her eyes red.

"Hello, old man!" said Terry and I fancied that his tone was not entirely cordial. "Just sit down and listen to this. We've been having some interesting disclosures."

Polly raised her head and cast him a reproachful glance, while with a limp wave of the hand she indicated a chair.

I settled myself and inquired reassuringly, "Well, Polly, what's the trouble?"

"You tell him," said Polly to Terry, as she settled herself to cry again.

"I'll tell you," said Terry, glancing warily at me, "but it's a secret, remember. You mustn't let any of those horrid newspaper men get hold of it. Miss Mathers would hate awfully to have anything like this get into the papers."

"Oh, go on, Terry," said I, crossly, "if you've got anything to tell, for heaven's sake tell it!"

"Well, as far as we'd got when you interrupted, was that that afternoon in the cave she and Radnor had somehow got separated from the rest of the party and gone on ahead. They sat down to wait for the others on the fallen column, and while they were waiting Radnor asked her to marry him, for the seventh—or was it the eighth time?"

"The seventh, I think," said Polly.

"It's happened so often that, she's sort of lost track; but anyway, she replied by asking him if he knew the truth about the ghost. He said, yes, he did, but he couldn't tell her; it was somebody else's secret. On his word of honor though there was nothing that he was to blame for. She said she wouldn't marry a man who had secrets. He said that unless she took him now, she would never have the chance again; it was the last time he was going to ask her—is that straight, Miss Mathers?"

"Y-yes," sobbed Polly from the depths of her cushion.

Terry proceeded with a fast broadening smile; it was evident that he enjoyed the recital.

"And then being naturally angry that any man should presume to propose for the last time, she proceeded to be 'perfectly horrid' to him.—Go on, Miss Mathers. That's as far as you'd got."

"I—I told him—you won't tell anyone?"

"No."

"I told him I'd decided to marry Jim Mattison."

"Ah—" said Terry. "Now we're getting at it! If you don't mind my asking, Miss Mathers, was that just a bluff on your part, or had Mr. Mattison really asked you?"

Polly sat up and eyed him with a sparkle of resentment.

"Certainly, he'd asked me—a dozen times."

"I beg pardon!" murmured Terry. "So now you're engaged to Mr. Mattison?"

"Oh, no!" cried Polly. "Jim doesn't know I said it—I didn't mean it; I just wanted to make Radnor mad."

"I see! So it was a bluff after all? Were you successful in making him mad?"

She nodded dismally.

"What did he say?"

"Oh, he was awfully angry! He said that if he never amounted to anything it would be my fault."

"And then what?"

"We heard the others coming and he started off. I called after him and asked him where he was going, and he said he was going to the d—devil."

Polly began to cry again, and Terry chuckled slightly.

"As a good many other young men have said under similar circumstances. But where he did go, was to the hotel; and there, it appears, he drank two glasses of brandy and swore at the stable boy.—Is that all, Miss Mathers?"

"Yes; it's the last time I ever saw him and he thinks I'm engaged to Jim Mattison."

"See here, Polly," said I with some excusable heat, "now why in thunder didn't you tell me all this before?"

"You didn't ask me."

"She was afraid that it would get into the papers," said Terry, soothingly. "It would be a terrible scandal to have anything like that get out. The fact that Radnor Gaylord was likely to be hanged for a murder he never committed, was in comparison a minor affair."

Polly turned upon him with a flash of gray eyes.

"I was going to tell before the trial. I didn't know the inquest made any difference. I would have told the coroner the morning he came to take my testimony, only he brought Jim Mattison with him as a witness, and I couldn't explain before Jim."

"That would have been awkward," Terry agreed.

"Polly," said I, severely. "This is inexcusable! If you had explained to me in the first place, the jury would never have remanded Radnor for trial."

"But I thought you would find the real murderer, and then Radnor would be set free. It would be awful to tell that story before a whole room full of people and have Jim Mattison hear it. I detest Jim Mattison!"

"Be careful what you say," said Terry. "You may have to take Jim Mattison after all. Radnor Gaylord will never ask you again."

"Then I'll ask him!" said Polly.

Terry laughed and rose.

"He's in a bad hole, Miss Mathers, but I'm not sure but that I envy him after all."

Polly dimpled through her tears; this was the language she understood.

"Good by," she said. "You'll remember your promise?"

"Never a syllable will I breathe," said Terry, and he put a hand on my shoulder and marched me off.

"She's a fascinating young person," he observed, as we turned into the road.

"You are not the first to discover that," said I.

"I fancy I'm not!" he retorted with a sidewise glance at me.

Terry gazed at the landscape a few moments with a pensive light in his eyes, then he threw back his head and laughed.

"Thank heaven, women don't go in for crime to any great extent! You're never safe in forming any theory about 'em—their motives and their actions don't match."

He paused to light a cigar and as soon as he got it well started took up the conversation again.

"It's just as I suspected in regard to Rad, though I will say the papers furnished mighty few clues. It was the coat that put me on the track coupled with his behavior at the hotel. You see his emotions when he came out of that cave were mixed. There was probably a good deal of disappointment and grief down below his anger, but that for the moment was decidedly in the lead. He had been badly treated, and he knew it. What's more, he didn't care who else knew it. He was in a thoroughly vicious mood and ready to wreak his anger on the first thing that came to hand. That happened to be his horse. By the time he got home he had expended the most of his temper and his disappointment had come to the top. You found him wrestling with that. By evening he had brought his philosophy into play, and had probably decided to brace up and try again. And that," he finished, "is the whole story of our young gentleman's erratic behavior."

"I wonder I didn't think of it myself," I said.

Terry smiled and said nothing.

"Radnor is naturally not loquacious about the matter," he resumed presently. "For one thing, because he does not wish to drag Polly's name into it, for another, I suppose he feels that if anyone is to do the explaining, she ought to be the one. He supposed that she would be present at the inquest and that her testimony would bring out sufficient facts to clear him. When he found that she was not there, and that her testimony did not touch on any important phase of the matter, he simply shut his mouth and said, 'Very well! If she won't tell, I won't.' Also, the coroner's manner was unfortunate. He showed that his sympathy was on the other side; and Radnor stubbornly determined not to say one word more than was dragged out of him by main force. It is much the attitude of the little boy who has been unfairly punished, and who derives an immense amount of satisfaction from the thought of how sorry his friends will be when he is dead. And now, I think we have Rad's case well in hand. In spite of the fact that he seems bound to be hung, we shall not have much difficulty in getting him off."

"But what I can't understand," I grumbled, "is why that little wretch didn't tell me a word of all this. She came and informed me off-hand that he was innocent and asked me to clear him, with never a hint that she could explain the most suspicious circumstance against him."

"You've got me," Terry laughed. "I give up when it comes to finding out why women do things. If you had *asked* her, you know, she would have told you; but you never said a word about it."

"How could I ask her when I didn't know anything about it?"

"I managed to ask her," said Terry, "and what's more," he added gloomily, "I promised it shouldn't go any further—that is, than is necessary to get Rad off. Now don't you call that pretty tough luck, after coming 'way down here just to find out the truth, not to be allowed to print it when I've got it? How in the deuce am I to account for Rad's behavior without mentioning her?"

"You needn't have promised," I suggested.

"Oh, well," Terry grinned, "I'm human!"

I let this pass and he added hastily, "We've disposed of Jeff; we've disposed of Radnor, but the real murderer is still to be found."

"And that," I declared, "is Cat-Eye Mose."

"It's possible," agreed Terry with a shrug. "But I have just the tiniest little entering wedge of a suspicion that the real murderer is not Cat-Eye Mose."

CHAPTER XXI

MR. TERENCE KIRKWOOD PATTEN OF NEW YORK

"There is Luray," I said, pointing with my whip to the scattered houses of the village as they lay in the valley at our feet.

Terry stretched out a hand and pulled the horses to a standstill. "Whoa, just a minute till I get my bearings. Now, in which direction is the cave?"

"It extends all along underneath us. The entrance is over there in the undergrowth about a mile to the east."

"And the woods extend straight across the mountain in an unbroken line?"

"Pretty much so. There are a few farms scattered in."

"How about the farmers? Are they well-to-do around here?"

"I think on the whole they are."

"Which do they employ mostly to work in the fields, negroes or white men?"

"As to that I can't say. It depends largely on circumstances. I think the smaller farms are more likely to employ white men."

"Let me see," said Terry, "this is just about planting time. Are the farmers likely to take on extra men at this season?"

"No, I don't think so; harvest time is when they are more likely to need help."

"Farming is new to me," laughed Terry. "East Side problems don't involve it. A man of Mose's habits could hide pretty effectually in those woods if he chose." He scanned the hills again and then brought his eyes back to the village. "I suppose we might as well go on to the hotel first. I should like to interview some of the people there. And by the way," he added, "it's as well not to let them know I'm a friend of yours—or a newspaper man either. I think I'll be a detective. Your young man from Washington seems to have made quite a stir in regard to the robbery; we'll see if I can't beat him. There's nothing that so impresses a rural population as a detective. They look upon him as omnipotent and omniscient, and every man squirms before him in the fear that his own little sins will be brought to light." Terry laughed in prospect. "Introduce me as a detective by all means!"

"Anything you like," I laughed in return. "I'll introduce you as the Pope if you think it will do any good." There was no keeping Terry suppressed, and his exuberance was contagious. I was beginning to feel light-hearted myself.

The hotel at Luray was a long rambling structure which had been casually added to from time to time. It was painted a sickly, mustard yellow (a color which, the landlord assured me, would last forever) but it's brilliancy was somewhat toned by a thick coating of dust. A veranda extended across the front of the building flush with the wooden side-walk. The veranda was furnished with a railing, and the railing was furnished at all times of the day—except for a brief nooning from twelve to half-past—with a line of boot-soles in assorted sizes.

We drew up with a flourish before the wooden steps in front of the hotel, and I threw the lines to the stable boy who came forward to receive us with an amusing air of importance. His connection with the Luray tragedy conferred a halo of distinction, and he realized the fact. It was not every one in the neighborhood who had had the honor of being cursed by a murderer. As we alighted Terry stopped to ask him a few questions. The boy had told his story to so many credulous audiences that by this time it was well-nigh unrecognizable. As he repeated it now for Terry's benefit, the evidence against Radnor appeared conclusive. A full confession of guilt could scarcely have been more damning.

Terry threw back his head and laughed.

"Take care, young man," he warned, "you'll be eating your

words one of these days, and some of them will be pretty hard to swallow."

As we mounted the steps I nodded to several of the men whom I remembered having seen before; and they returned an interested, "How-dy-do? Pleasant day," as they cast a reconnoitering glance at my companion.

"Gentlemen," I said with a wave of my hand toward Terry, "let me introduce Mr. Terence Kirkwood Patten, the well-known detective of New York, who has come down to look into this matter for us."

The chairs which were tipped back against the wall came down with a thud, and an awed and somewhat uneasy shuffling of feet ensued.

"I wish to go through the cave," Terry remarked in the crisp, incisive tones a detective might be supposed to employ, "and I should like to have the same guide who conducted Mr. Crosby the time the body was discovered."

"That's Pete Moser, he's out in the back lot plowin'," a half dozen voices responded.

"Ah, thank you; will some one kindly call him? We will wait here."

Terry proceeded with his usual ease to make himself at home. He tipped back his hat, inclined his chair at the same dubious angle as the others, and ranged his feet along the railing. He produced cigars from various pockets, and the atmosphere became less strained. They were beginning to realize that detectives are made of the same flesh and blood as other people. I gave Terry the lead—perhaps it would be more accurate to say that he took it—but it did not strike me that he set about his interviewing in a very business-like manner. He did not so much as refer to the case we had come to investigate, but chatted along pleasantly about the weather and the crops and the difficulty of finding farm-hands.

We had not been settled very long when, to my surprise, Jim Mattison strolled out from the bar-room. What he was doing in

Luray, I could easily conjecture. Mattison's assumption of interest in the case all along had angered me beyond measure. It is not, ordinarily, a part of the sheriff's duties to assist the prosecution in making out a case against one of his prisoners; and owing to the peculiar relation he bore to Radnor, his interference was not only bad law but excruciatingly bad taste. My dislike of the man had grown to such an extent that I could barely be civil to him. It was only because it was policy on my part not to make him an active enemy that I tolerated his presence at all.

I presented Terry; though Mattison took his calling more calmly than the others, still I caught several sidewise glances in his direction, and I think he was impressed.

"Happy to know you, Mr. Patten," he remarked as he helped himself to a chair and settled it at the general angle. "This is a pretty mysterious case in some respects. I rode over myself this morning to look into a few points and I shall be glad to have some help—though I'm afraid we'll not find anything that'll please you."

"Anything pleases me, so long as it's the truth," Terry threw off, as he studied the sheriff, with a gleam of amusement in his eyes; he was thinking, I knew, of Polly Mathers. "I hope," he added, assuming a severely professional tone, "that you haven't let a lot of people crowd into the cave and tramp up all the marks."

The landlord, who was standing in the doorway, chuckled at this.

"There ain't many people that you could drive into that there cave at the point of the pistol," he assured us. "They think it's haunted; leastways the niggers do."

"Have niggers been in the habit of going in much?"

"Oh, more or less," the sheriff returned, "when they want to make themselves inconspicuous for any reason. I had a horse thief hide in there for two weeks last year while we were scouring the country for him. There are so many little holes; it's almost impossible to find a man. Tramps occasionally spend the night there in cold weather."

"Do you have many tramps around here?"

"Not a great many. Once in a while a nigger comes along and asks for something to eat."

"More often he takes it without asking," one of the men broke in. "A week or so ago my ole woman had a cheese an' a ham an' two whole pies that she'd got ready for a church social just disappear without a word, out o' the pantry winder. If that ain't the mark of a nigger, I miss my guess."

Terry laughed.

"If that happened in the North we should look around the neighborhood for a sick small boy."

"It wasn't no boy this time—leastways not a very small one," the man affirmed, "for that same day a pair o' my boots that I'd left in the wood house just naturally walked off by theirselves, an' I found 'em the next day at the bottom o' the pasture. It would take a pretty sizeable fellow that my boots was too small for," he finished with a grin.

"They *are* a trifle conspicuous," one of the others agreed with his eyes on the feet in question.

I caught an interested look in Terry's glance as he mentally took their measure, and I wondered what he was up to; but as our messenger and Pete Moser appeared around the corner at the moment, I had no time for speculation. Terry let his chair slip with a bang and rose to his feet.

"Ah, Mr. Moser! I'm glad to see you," he exclaimed with an air of relief. "It's getting late," he added, looking at his watch, "and I must get this business settled as soon as possible; I have another little affair waiting for me in New York. Bring plenty of calcium light, please. We want to see what we're doing."

As the four of us were preparing to start, Terry paused on the top step and nodded pleasantly to the group on the veranda.

"Thank you for your information, gentlemen. I have no doubt but that it will be of the greatest importance," and he turned away with a laugh at their puzzled faces.

The sheriff and I were equally puzzled. I should have suspected that Terry, in the rôle of detective, was playing a joke on them, had he not very evidently got something on his mind. He was of a sudden in a frenzy of impatience to reach the cave, and he kept well ahead of us most of the way.

"I suppose," said Mattison as he climbed a fence with tantalizing deliberation—we were going by way of the fields as that was shorter—"I suppose that you are trying to prove that Radnor Gaylord had nothing to do with this murder?"

"That will be easy enough," Terry threw back over his shoulder. "I dropped *him* long ago. The one I'm after now is the real murderer."

Mattison scowled slightly.

"If you can explain what it was that happened in that cave that upset him so mightily, I'd come a little nearer to believing you."

Terry laughed and fell back beside him.

"It's a thing which I imagine may have happened to one or two other young men of this neighborhood—not inconceivably yourself included."

Mattison, seeing no meaning in this sally, preserved a sulky silence and Terry added:

"The thing for us to do now is to bend all our energies toward finding Cat-Eye Mose. I doubt if we can completely explain the mystery until he is discovered."

"And that," said the sheriff, "will be never! You may mark my words; whoever killed the Colonel, killed Mose, too."

"It's possible," said Terry with an air of sadness, "but I hope not. I came all the way down from New York on purpose to see Mose, and I should hate to miss him."

CHAPTER XXII

THE DISCOVERY OF CAT-EYE MOSE

Having lighted our candles, we descended into the cave and set out along the path I now knew so well. When we reached the pool the guide lit a calcium light which threw a fierce white glare over the little body of water and the limestone cliffs, and even penetrated to the stalactite draped roof far above our heads. For a moment we stood blinking our eyes scarcely able to see, so sudden was the change from the semi-darkness of our four flickering candles. Then Terry stepped forward.

"Show me where you found the body and point out the spot where the struggle took place."

He spoke in quick, eager tones, so excited that he almost stuttered. It was not necessary for him to act the part of detective any longer. He had forgotten that he ever was a reporter—he had forgotten almost that he was a human being.

From where we stood we pointed out the place above the pool where the struggle had occurred, the spot under the cliff where the body had lain, and the jagged piece of rock on which we had found the coat. Moser even laid down upon the ground and spread out his arms in the position in which we had discovered the Colonel's body.

"Very well, I see," said Terry. "Now the rest of you stay back there on the boards; I don't want you to make a mark."

He stepped forward carefully to the edge of the water and bent over to examine the soft, yellow clay which formed the border of the pool on the lower side. Instantly he straightened up with a sharp exclamation of surprise.

"Did any negroes come in with you to recover the body?" he asked.

"No," returned the sheriff, "as old man Tompkins said, you couldn't hire a nigger to stick his head in here after the Colonel was found. They say they can hear something wailing around the pool and they think his ghost is haunting it."

"They can hear something wailing, can they?" Terry repeated queerly. "Well I begin to believe they can! What is the meaning of this?" he demanded, facing around at us. "How do you account for these peculiar foot-prints?"

"What prints?" I asked as we all pressed forward.

At the moment the calcium light with a final flare, died out, and we were left again in the flickering candle light which seemed darkness to us now.

"Quick, touch off another calcium!" said Terry, with suppressed impatience. He laid a hand on my shoulder and my arm ached from the tightness of his grip. "There," he said pointing with his finger as the light flared up again. "What do you make of those?"

I bent over and plainly traced the prints of bare feet, going and coming and over-lapping one another, just as an animal would make in pacing a cage. I shivered slightly. It was a terribly uncanny sight.

"Well?" said Terry sharply. The place was beginning to get on his nerves too.

"Terry," I said uneasily, "I never saw them before. I thought I examined everything thoroughly, but I was so excited I suppose—"

"What did you make of them?" he interrupted, whirling about on Mattison who was looking over our shoulders.

"I—I didn't see them," Mattison stammered.

"For heaven's sake, men," said Terry impatiently. "Do you mean they weren't there or you didn't notice them?"

The sheriff and I looked at each other blankly, and neither answered.

Terry stood with his hands in his pockets frowning down at the marks, while the rest of us waited silently, scarcely daring to think. Finally he turned away without saying a word, and, motioning us to keep back, commenced examining the path which led up the incline. He mounted the three stone steps, and with his eyes on the ground, slowly advanced to the spot where the struggle had taken place.

"How tall a man did you say Mose was?" he called down to us.

"Little short fellow—not more than five feet high," returned the sheriff.

Terry took his ruler from his pocket and bent over to study the marks at the scene of the struggle. He straightened up with an air of satisfaction.

"Now I want you men to look carefully at those marks on the lower borders of the pool, and then come up here and look at these. Come along up in single file, please, and keep to the middle of the path."

He spoke in the tone of one giving a demonstration before a kindergarten class. We obeyed him silently and ranged in a row along the boards.

"Come here," he said. "Bend over where you can see. Now look at those marks. Do you see anything different in them from the marks below?"

The sheriff and I gazed intently at the prints of bare feet which marked the entire vicinity of the struggle. We had both examined them more than once before, and we saw nothing now but what had already appeared. We straightened up and shook our heads.

"They're the prints of bare feet," said Mattison, stolidly. "But I don't see that they're any different from any other bare feet."

Terry handed him the ruler.

"Measure them," he said. "Measure this one that's flat on the ground. Now go down and measure one of those prints by the borders of the pool."

Mattison took the ruler and complied. As he bent over the

marks on the lower border we could see by the light of his candle the look of astonishment that sprang into his face.

"Well, what do you find?" Terry asked.

"The marks up there are nearly two inches longer and an inch broader."

"Exactly."

"Terry," I said, "you can't blame us for not finding that out. We examined everything when we took away the body, and those marks below were simply not there. Someone has been in since."

"So I conclude. Now, Mattison," he added to the sheriff, "come here and show me the marks of Radnor Gaylord's riding boots."

Mattison returned and pointed out the mark which he had produced at the inquest, but his assurance, I noticed, was somewhat shaken.

"That," said Terry half contemptuously, "is the mark of Colonel Gaylord. You must remember that he was struggling with his assailant. He did not plant his foot squarely every time. Sometimes we have only the heel mark: sometimes only the toe. In this case we have more than the mark of the whole foot. How do I account for it? Simply enough. The Colonel's foot slipped sideways. The mark is, you see, exactly the same in length as the others, but disproportionately broad. At the heel and toe it is smudged, and on the inside where the weight was thrown, it is heavier than on the outside. The thing is easy enough to understand. You ought to have been able to deduce it for yourselves. And besides, how did you account for the fact that there was only one mark? A man engaged in a struggle must have left more than that behind him. No; it is quite clear. At this point on the edge of the bank there was no third person. We are dealing with only two men—Colonel Gaylord and his murderer; and the murderer was bare-footed."

"Mose?" I asked.

"No," said Terry, patiently, "not Mose."

"Then who?"

"That—remains to be seen. I will follow him up and find out

where he comes from."

Terry held his candle close to the ground and followed along the path. At the entrance to the little gallery of the broken column it diverged, one part leading into the gallery, and the other into a sort of blind alley at one side. Terry paused at the opening.

"Give me some more calcium light," he called to the guide. "I want to look into this passage. And just hand me some of those boards," he added. "It's very necessary that we keep the marks clear."

The rest of us stood in a huddled group on the one or two boards he had left us and watched him curiously as he made his way down the passage. He paused at the end and examined the ground. We saw him stoop and pick up something. Then he rose quickly with a cry of triumph and came running back to us holding his hands behind him.

"It's just as I suspected," he said, his eyes shining with excitement. "Colonel Gaylord had an enemy he did not know."

"What do you mean?" we asked, crowding around.

"Here's the proof," and he held out towards us a well gnawed ham bone in one hand and a cheese rind in the other. "These were the provisions intended for the church social; the pies, I fancy, have disappeared."

We stared at him a moment in silent wonder. The sheriff was the first to assert himself.

"What have these to do with the crime?" he asked, viewing the trophies with an air of disgust.

"Everything. The man who stole those is the man who robbed the safe and who murdered Colonel Gaylord."

The sheriff uttered a low laugh of incredulity, and the guide and I stared open-mouthed.

"And what's more, I will tell you what he looks like. He is a large, very black negro something over six feet tall. When last seen, he was dressed in a blue and white checked blouse and ragged overalls. His shoes were much the worse for wear, and have since been thrown away. He was bare-footed at the time he committed the crime. In short," Terry added, "he is the chicken thief whom Colonel Gaylord whipped a couple of days before he died," and he briefly repeated the incident I had told him.

"You mean," I asked, "that he was the ha'nt?"

"Yes," said Terry, "he was the second ha'nt. He has been hiding for two or three weeks in the spring-hole at Four-Pools, keeping hidden during the day and coming out at night to prowl around and steal whatever he could lay his hands on. He doubtless deserved punishment, but that fact would not make him the less bitter over the Colonel's beating. When I heard that story, I said to myself, 'there is a man who would be ready for revenge if chance put the opportunity in his way.'"

"But," I expostulated, "how did he happen to be in the cave?"

"As to that I cannot say. After the Colonel's beating he probably did not dare to hang about Four-Pools any longer. He took to the woods and came in this direction; being engaged in petty thieving about the neighborhood, it was necessary to find a hiding place during the daytime and the cave was his most natural refuge. We know that he is not afraid of the dark—the spring-hole at Four-Pools is about as dismal a place as a man could find. He established himself in this passage in order to be near the water. See, here in the corner are drops of candle grease and the remains of a fire. On the day of the Mathers's picnic he doubtless saw the party pass through and recognized Colonel Gaylord. It brought to his mind the thrashing he had received. While he was still brooding over the matter, the Colonel came back alone, and it flashed into the fellow's mind that this was his chance. He may have been afraid at first or he may have hesitated through kindlier motives. At any rate he did not attack the Colonel immediately, but retreated into the passage, and the old man passed him without seeing him and went on into the gallery and got the coat.

"In the meantime, the negro had made up his mind, and as the Colonel came back, he crept along behind him. It is hard to trace the marks, for another bare-footed man has walked over them since. But see, in this place at the edge of the path, there's the mark of a palm, showing where the assassin's hand rested when he crouched on the ground. He sprang upon the old man from the rear and they struggled together over the water—touch off a light, please—you see how the clay is all trampled over on both sides of the path, 'way out to the brink of the pool. There is no second set of marks here to obliterate it; we are dealing with just two people—Colonel Gaylord and his assassin."

Terry bent low and picked up from a crevice what looked like a piece of stone covered with clay.

"Here, you see, is the end of the Colonel's candle. He probably dropped it when the man first sprang, and in the darkness he could not tell who or what had attacked him. In his frenzy to have a light he snatched out his match box—Radnor's box—and that too was dropped in the scuffle.

"Now, even if the original motive of the crime were not robbery but revenge—as I fancy it was—at any rate the murderer, being a tramp and a thief, would have robbed the body. But he did not. Why was that? Because he saw or heard something that frightened him, and what could that have been but Mose running to his master's assistance?"

Terry strode over to the steps which led to the incline, and motioning us to follow, pointed out some marks on the sloping bank at the side of the path.

"See, here are Mose's tracks. He was in such a hurry that he could not wait to come up by the steps; he tried to take a cross cut. He scrambled up the slippery bank so fast that he fell on his hands and knees in this place and slid back. That accounts for those long dragging marks, which none of you appear to have noticed. Mose did his best, but he could not reach his master in time. The murderer seeing—or rather hearing him, for it must have been dark—was seized with sudden fear, and with a convulsive effort he threw the old man against the rock wall here, where his head struck on this broken stalactite. If you look carefully you can see the marks of blood. He then hurled him into the pool and fled."

"It sounds plausible enough," said the sheriff slowly, "but there are one or two points which I'm afraid will not bear examining. Suppose your man did thrown the Colonel into the water and run for it, then what, I should like to know, has become of Cat-Eye Mose?"

"That," said Terry, knitting his brows, "is still a mystery and a fairly deep one. There is something uncommonly strange about those tracks on the lower borders of the pool and I confess they puzzle me. Only one explanation occurs to me now and that is not pleasant to think of. We have some clues to work with however, and we ought not to be long in getting at the truth. If I had had your chance of examining the cave on the day of the crime," he added, "I think I should know."

"You might, and again you might not," said Mattison. "It's easy enough for you fellows to come down here and make up a story about a lot of people you've never seen, but I'll tell you one thing, and that is that you're not so likely to hit the truth as the men who've been brought up in the country. In the first place it comes natural to niggers to be whipped and they don't mind it. In the second place if your tramp *did* want to take it out on the Colonel why should he be scared by Mose, who was a little bit of a sawed-off cuss that I could lick with one hand tied behind me? You may be able to impress a New York jury with a ham bone and a cheese rind, Mr. Patten, but I can tell you, sir, that a Virginia jury wants witnesses."

"We shall do our best to provide some," said Terry, coolly.

"And perhaps you can tell," added Mattison with the triumphant air of clinching the matter, "what has become of the five thousand dollars in bonds? You can never make me believe that any nigger—"

"Oh, they're back in the safe at Four-Pools. I found 'em this morning in the spring-hole where the man had thrown them away.—Now, gentlemen," he added with a touch of impatience,

"I want to try a little experiment before we leave the cave. Will you all please put out your lights? I want to see how dark it really is in here."

We blew out our candles and stood a moment in silence. At first all was black around us, but as our eyes became accustomed to the darkness, we saw that a faint light filtered in from somewhere in the roof above our heads. We could make out the pale blur of the white rock wall on one side and the merest glimmer of the pool below.

"No," Terry began, "he could have seen nothing; he must have—" He broke off suddenly and gripping my arm whispered out, "What's that?"

"Where?" I asked.

"Up there; straight ahead."

I looked up and saw two round eyes which glittered like a wild beast's, staring at us out of the darkness. A cold chill ran up my back and I instinctively huddled closer to the others. For a moment no one spoke and I heard the click of Terry's revolver as he cocked it. Then it suddenly came over me what it was, and I cried out:

"It's Cat-Eye Mose!"

"Good Lord, he can see in the dark! Strike a light, some one," Terry said huskily.

The sheriff struck a match. We lit our candles with trembling hands and pressed forward (in a body) to the spot where the eyes had appeared.

Crouched in a corner of a little recess half way up the irregular wall, we found Mose, shivering with fear and looking down at us with dumb, animal eyes. We had to drag him out by main force. The poor fellow was nearly famished and so weak he could scarcely stand. What little sense he had ever possessed seemed to have left him, and he jabbered in a tongue that was scarcely English.

We bolstered him up with a few drops of whisky from Mattison's flask, and half carried him out into the light. The guide ran ahead to get a carriage, spreading the news as he ran, that Cat-Eye Mose had been found. Half the town of Luray came out to the cave to escort us back, and I think the feeling of regret was general, in that there had not been time enough to collect a brass band.

CHAPTER XXIII

MOSE TELLS HIS STORY

We took Mose back to the hotel, shut out the crowd, and gave him something to eat. He was quite out of his head and it was only by dint of the most patient questioning that we finally got his story. It was, in substance, as Terry had sketched it in the cave.

In obedience to my request, Mose had gone back after the coat, not knowing that the Colonel was before him. Suddenly, as he came near the pool he heard a scream and looked up in time to see a big negro—the one my uncle had struck with his crop—spring upon the Colonel with the cry, "It's my tu'n, now, Cunnel Gaylord. You whup me, an' I'll let you see what it feels like."

The Colonel turned and clinched with his assailant, and in the struggle the light was dropped. Mose, with a cry, ran forward to his master's assistance, but when the negro saw him climbing up the bank he suddenly screamed, and hurling the old man from him, turned and fled.

"The fellow must have taken him for the devil when he saw those eyes, and I don't wonder!" Terry interpolated at this point.

After the Colonel's murder, it seems that Mose, crazed by grief and fear, had watched us carry the body away, and then had stayed by the spot where his master had died. This accounted for the marks on the border of the pool. Knowing all of the intricate passages and hiding places as he did, it had been an easy matter for him to evade the party that had searched for his body. He ate the food the murderer had left, but this being exhausted, he would, I haven't a doubt, have died there himself with the unreasoning faithfulness of a dog.

When he finished his rambling and in some places scarcely intelligible account, we sat for a moment with our eyes upon his face, fascinated by his look. Every bit of repugnance I had ever felt toward him had vanished, and there was left in its place only a sense of pity. Mose's cheeks were hollow, his features sharper than ever, and his face was almost pale. From underneath his straight, black, matted hair his eyes glittered feverishly, and their expression of uncomprehending anguish was pitiful to see. He seemed like a dumb animal that has come into contact with death for the first time and asks the reason.

Terry took his eyes from Mose's face and looked down at the table with a set jaw. I do not think that he was deriving as much pleasure from the sight as he had expected. We all of us experienced a feeling of relief when the doctor appeared at the door. We turned Mose over to him with instructions to do what he could for the poor fellow and to take him back to Four-Pools.

As the door shut behind them, the sheriff said (with a sigh, I thought), "This business proves one thing: it's never safe to lynch a man until you are sure of the facts."

"It proves another thing," said Terry, dryly, "which is a thing you people don't seem to have grasped; and that is that negroes are human beings and have feelings like the rest of us. Poor old Colonel Gaylord paid a terrible price for not having learned it earlier in life."

We pondered this in silence for a moment, then the sheriff voiced a feeling which, to a slight extent, had been lurking in the background of my own consciousness, in spite of my relief at the dénouement.

"It's kind of disappointing when you've got your mind worked up to something big, to find in the end that there was nothing but a chance nigger at the bottom of all that mystery. Seems sort of a let-down."

Terry eyed him with an air of grim humor, then he leaned across the table and spoke with a ring of conviction that carried his message home.

"You are mistaken, Mattison, the murderer of Colonel Gaylord was not a chance nigger. There was no chance about it. Colonel Gaylord killed himself. He committed suicide—as truly as if he had blown out his brains with a gun. He did it with his uncontrollable temper. The man was an egoist. He has always looked upon his own desires and feelings as of supreme importance. He has tried to crush the life and spirit and independence from everyone about him. But once too often he wreaked his anger upon an innocent person—at least upon a person that for all he knew was innocent—and at one stroke his past injustices were avenged. It was not chance that killed Colonel Gaylord. It was the inevitable law of cause and effect. 'Way back in his boyhood when he gave way to his first fit of passion, he sentenced himself to some such end as this. Every unjust act in his after-life piled up the score against him.

"Oh, I've seen it a hundred times! It's character that tells. I've seen it happen to a political boss—a man whose business it was to make friends with every voter high and low. I've seen him forget, just once, and turn on a man, humiliate him, wound his pride, crush him under foot and think no more of the matter than if he had stepped on a worm. And I've seen that man, the most insignificant of the politician's followers, work and plot and scheme to overthrow him; and in the end succeed. The big man never knew what struck him. He thought it was luck, chance, a turn of the wheel. He never dreamed that it was his own character hitting back. I've seen it so often, I'm a fatalist. I don't believe in chance. It was Colonel Gaylord who killed himself, and he commenced it fifty years ago."

"It's God's own truth, Terry!" I said solemnly.

The sheriff had listened to Terry's words with an anxiously reminiscent air. I wondered if he were reviewing his own political past, to see if by chance he also had unwittingly crushed a worm. He raised his eyes to Terry's face with a gleam of admiration.

"You've been pretty clever, Mr. Patten, in finding out the truth about this crime," he acknowledged generously. "But you couldn't have expected me to find out," he added, "for I didn't know any of the circumstances. I had never even heard that such a man existed as that chicken thief—and as to there being two ghosts instead of one, there wasn't a suggestion of it brought out at the inquest."

Terry looked at him with his usual slowly broadening smile. He opened his mouth to say something, but he changed his mind and—with a visible effort—shut it again.

"Terry," I asked, "how *did* you find out about the chicken thief? I confess I don't understand it yet."

He shrugged his shoulders and laughed.

"Nothing simpler. The trouble with you people was that you were searching for something lurid, and the little common-place things which, in a case like this, are the most suggestive, you overlooked. As soon as I read the story of the crime in the papers I saw that in all probability Rad was innocent. His behavior was far too suspicious for him really to be guilty; unless he were a fool he would have covered up his tracks. There was of course the possibility that Mose had committed the murder, but in the light of his past devotion to the Colonel it did not seem likely.

"I had already been reading a lot of sensational stuff about the ghost of Four-Pools, and when the murder followed so close on the heels of the robbery, I commenced to look about for a connecting link. It was evident that Radnor had nothing to do with it, but whether or not he suspected someone was not so clear. His reticence in regard to the ha'nt made me think that he did. I came South with pretty strong suspicions against the elder son, but with a mind still open to conviction. The telegram showing that he was in Seattle at the time of the murder, proved his innocence of that, but he might still be connected with the ha'nt. I tried the suggestion on Radnor, and his manner of taking it proved pretty conclusively that I had stumbled on the truth. The ha'nt business, I dare say, was started as a joke, and was kept up as being a convenient method of warding off eavesdroppers. Why Jefferson came back and why Radnor gave him money are not matters that concern us; if they prefer to keep it a secret that's their own affair.

"Jeff helped himself pretty freely to cigars, roast chickens, jam, pajamas, books, brandy, and anything else he needed to make himself comfortable in the cabin, but he took nothing of any great value. In the meantime, though, other things commenced disappearing—things that Radnor knew his brother had no use for—and he supposed the workers about the place were stealing and laying it to the ghost, as a convenient scapegoat.

"But as a matter of fact they were not. A second ghost had appeared on the scene. This tramp negro had taken up his quarters in the spring-hole and was prowling about at night seeking what he might devour. He ran across Jeff dressed in a sheet, and decided to do some masquerading on his own account. Sheets were no longer left on the line all night, so he had to put up with lap robes. As a result, the spring-hole shortly became haunted by a jet black spirit nine feet tall with blue flames and sulphur, and all the other accessories.

"This made little impression at the house until Mose himself was frightened; then Radnor saw that the hoax had reached the point where it was no longer funny, and he determined to get rid of Jeff immediately. While he drove him to the station he left Mose behind to straighten up the loft; and Mose, coming into the house to put some things away, met ghost number two just after he had robbed the safe. If Mose's eyes looked as they did to-day I fancy the fright was mutual. The ghost, in his excitement, dropped one package of papers, but bolted with the rest. He made for his lair in the spring-hole and examined his booty. The bonds were no more than old paper; he tossed them aside. But the pennies and five-cent pieces were real; he lit out for the village with them. The robbery was not discovered till morning and by that time the fellow was at 'Jake's place' on his way toward being the drunkest nigger in the county.

"He stayed at the Corners a week or so until the money was gone, then he came back to the spring-hole. But he made the mistake of venturing out by daylight; the stable-men caught him and took him to the Colonel, and you know the rest.

"As soon as I heard the story of the beating I decided to follow it up; and when I heard of a jet black spirit rising from the spring-hole, I decided to follow that up too. At daylight this morning I routed out one of the stable-men, and we went down and examined the spring-hole; at least I examined it while he stood outside and shivered. It yielded an even bigger find than I had hoped for. Chucked off in a corner and trampled with mud I found the bonds. A pile of clothing and carriage cushions formed a bed. There were the remains of several fires and of a great many chickens—the whole place was strewn with feathers and bones; he had evidently raided the roosts more than once.

"When I finished with the spring-hole it still lacked something of six o'clock and I rode over to the village hoping to get an answer to my telegram. I wanted to get Jeff's case settled. 'Miller's store' was not open but 'Jake's place' was, and it was not long before I got on the track of my man. There was no doubt but that I had him accounted for up to the time of the thrashing; after that I could only conjecture. He had not appeared in the village again; the supposition was that he had taken to the woods. Now he might or he might not have come in the direction of Luray. All the facts I had to go upon were, a man of criminal proclivities, who owed Colonel Gaylord a grudge, and who was used to hiding in caves. It was pure supposition that he had come in this direction and it had to be checked at every point by fact. I didn't mention my suspicions because there was no use in raising false hopes and because, well—"

"You wanted to be dramatic," I suggested.

"Oh, yes, certainly, that's my business. Well, anyway I felt I was getting warm, and I came over here this morning with my eyes open, ready to see what there was to see.

"The first thing I unearthed was this story of the church social provisions. There had, then, been a thief of some sort in the neighborhood just at the time of Colonel Gaylord's murder.

The further theft of the boots fitted very neatly into the theory. If the fellow had been tramping for a couple of days his shoes, already worn, had given out and been discarded. The new ones, as we know, were too small—he left them at the bottom of the pasture—and went bare-footed. The marks therefore in the cave, which everyone ascribed to Mose, were in all probability, not the marks of Mose at all. Actual investigation proved that to be the case. The rest, I think, you know. The Four-Pools mystery has turned out to be a very simple affair—as most mysteries unfortunately do."

"I reckon you're a pretty good detective, Mr. Patten," said Mattison with a shade of envy in his voice.

Terry bowed his thanks and laughed.

"As a matter of fact," he returned, "I am not a detective of any sort—at least not officially. I merely assume the part once in a while when there seems to be a demand. Officially," he added, "I am the representative of the New York Post-Dispatch, a paper which, you may know, has solved a good many mysteries before now. In this case, the Post-Dispatch will of course take the credit, but it wants a little more than that. It wants to be the only paper tomorrow morning to print the true details. We four are the only ones who know them. I should, perhaps, have been a little more circumspect, and kept the facts to myself, but I knew that I could trust you."

His eye dwelt upon the sheriff a moment and then wandered to Pete Moser who had sat silently listening throughout the colloquy.

"Would it be too much," Terry inquired, "to ask you to keep silent until tomorrow morning?"

"You can trust me to keep quiet," said Mattison, holding out his hand.

"Me too," said Moser. "I reckon I can make up something that'll satisfy the boys about as well as the real thing."

"Thank you," Terry said. "I guess you can all right! There doesn't seem to be anything the matter with your imaginations down here."

"And now," said Mattison, rising, "I suppose the first thing, is to see about Radnor's release, though I swear I don't know yet what was the matter with him on the day of the crime."

"I believe you have the honor of Miss Polly Mathers's acquaintance? Perhaps she will enlighten you," suggested Terry.

A look of illumination flashed over Mattison's face. Terry laughed and rose.

"I have a reason for suspecting that Miss Mathers has changed her mind and, if it is not too irregular, I should like by way of payment to drive her to the Kennisburg jail myself and let her be the first to tell him—I want to give her a reason for remembering me."

CHAPTER XXIV

POLLY MAKES A PROPOSAL

I was dropped in Kennisburg to attend to the legal formalities respecting Radnor's release, while Terry appropriated the horses and drove to Mathers Hall. His last word to Mattison and me was not to let a whisper reach Radnor's ear as to the outcome of the investigation. He wanted a spectacular dénouement. The sheriff assented very soberly. The truth had at last forced itself upon him that his chances with Polly were over.

Terry reappeared, two hours later, with a very excited young woman beside him. They joined us in the bare little parlor of the jail, and if Mattison needed any further proof that the end had come, Polly's greeting furnished it. An embarrassed flush rose to her face as she saw him, but she shook hands in a studiously impersonal way and asked immediately for Radnor.

Mattison met the situation with a dignity I had scarcely expected. He called a deputy and turned us over to him; and with the remark that his services were happily no longer needed, he bowed himself out. I saw him two minutes later recklessly galloping down the street. Polly's eyes, also, followed the rider, and for a second I detected a shade of remorse.

As we climbed the stairs Terry fell back and whispered to me, "I tell you, I laid down the law coming over; we'll see if she's game."

As the door of the cell was thrown open, Rad raised his head and regarded us with a look of bewildered astonishment. Polly walked straight in and laid her hand on his shoulder.

"Radnor," she said, "you told me you would never ask me

again to marry you. Did you really mean it?"

Rad still stared confusedly from her to Terry and me.

"Well!" Polly sighed. "If you did mean it, then I suppose I'll have to ask you. Will you marry me, Radnor?"

I laid a hand on Terry's arm and backed him, much against his will, into the corridor.

"Jove! You don't suppose he's going to refuse her?" he inquired in a stage whisper.

"No such luck," I laughed.

We took a couple of turns up and down the corridor and cautiously presented ourselves in the doorway. Polly was telling, between laughing and crying, the story of Mose's discovery. Radnor came to meet us, his left arm still around Polly, his right hand extended to Terry.

"Will you shake hands, Patten?" he asked. "I'm afraid I wasn't very decent, but you know—"

"Oh, that's no matter," said Terry, easily. "I wasn't holding it up against you. But I hope you realize, Gaylord, that it's owing to me you've won Miss Mathers. She never would have got up the courage to ask you, if—"

"Yes, I should!" flashed Polly. "I wanted him too much ever to let him slip through my fingers again."

Terry's boast came true and Radnor dined at Four-Pools Plantation that night. The news of his release had in some way preceded us, and as we drove up to the house, all the negroes came crowding out on the portico to welcome home "young Marse Rad." But the one person who—whatever the circumstances—had always been first to welcome him back, was missing; and the poor boy felt his home-coming a very barren festival.

Terry was steadfast in the assertion that he had an engagement in New York the next day, and as soon as supper was over I drove him to the station. He was in an ecstatically self-satisfied frame of mind.

"Do you know I'm a pretty all-round fellow," he observed in a burst of confidence. "I've always known better than the proprietor how the paper ought to be run, and I can give the police points about detective work. I'm something of a cook, and I can play the hand-organ like Paderewski; but this is the first time I ever tried my hand at matchmaking and it comes as easy as a murder mystery!"

"You think that their engagement is due to you?"

"But isn't it? If it weren't for me they'd have it all to go over again from the beginning, and there's no telling how long they'd take about it."

"I hope they appreciate your services, Terry. You're so modest that what you do is in danger of being overlooked."

"They appreciate me fast enough," returned Terry, imperturbably. "I promised Polly to spend my first vacation with 'em after they're married—Oh, you'll see; I'll make a farmer one of these days!"

I laughed and then said seriously:

"Whether you made the marriage or not, you have cleared Radnor's name from any suspicion of dishonor, and I don't know how we can ever sufficiently show our gratitude."

"That's all right," said Terry with a deprecatory wave of his hand. "I enjoyed it. Never did anything just like it before. I've arranged a good many funerals of one sort or another, but this is the first time I ever arranged a marriage. And Jove! but I could make a story out of it," he added regretfully, "if she'd only let me tell the truth."

The events which I have chronicled happened a number of years ago, and Four-Pools has never since figured in the papers. I trust that its public life is ended. In spite of the most far-reaching search, the murderer of Colonel Gaylord was never found. Radnor and I have always believed that he was lynched by a mob in West Virginia some two years later. The description of the man tallied exactly with the appearance of the tramp my uncle had thrashed, and something he said in his ante-mortem statement, made us very sure of the fact.

Mose, until the time of his death, was an honored member

of the household, but he did not long outlive the Colonel. The memory of the tragedy he had witnessed seemed to follow him constantly; an unreasoning terror looked from his eyes, and he started and shivered at every sound. The poor fellow had lost what few wits he had ever possessed, but the one rational gleam that stayed with him to the end, was his love for his old master. When he lay dying. Radnor tells me, he roused after hours of unconsciousness, to call the Colonel's name. I have always felt that this devotion spoke equally well for both of them. The old man must have had some splendid traits underneath his crusty exterior to awaken such unquestioning love in a person of Mose's instinctive perceptions. Perhaps after all, half idiot though he was, Mose could see clearer than the rest of us. He now lies in the little family burying-ground on the edge of the plantation, a stone's throw from the grave of Colonel Gaylord.

There has never been any further rumor of a ha'nt at Four-Pools, and we hope that the family ghost is laid forever. The deserted cabins have been torn down, and the fourth pool dredged and confined, prosaically enough, within its banks. Its mysterious charm is gone, but it yields, every season, some fifteen barrels of watercress.

It was the following April—a year from the time of my first visit—that Terry and I snatched a couple of days from our work, purchased new frock coats, and served as ushers at Polly's wedding. She and Radnor have been living happily at Four-Pools ever since, and the house with a young mistress is a very different place from the house as it used to be. Marriage and responsibility have improved Radnor immensely. He has developed from a recklessly headstrong boy into a keen, rational, upright man; I am sure that Polly has never for a moment had cause to regret her choice.

When the estate was settled, Radnor, very justly, insisted on breaking his father's will and giving to Jeff his rightful share of the property. Jeff has since become middle-aged and respectable. He owns a raisin ranch in southern California with fifty Chinamen to run it. When he comes back to Four-Pools Plantation on an occasional visit, he occupies the guest room.

www.ingramcontent.com/pod-product-compliance
Lightning Source LLC
LaVergne TN
LVHW091149080826
845145LV00008B/2305
* 9 7 8 1 5 2 8 7 1 1 7 4 6 *